SIMON

BAYOU BROTHERHOOD PROTECTORS
BOOK EIGHT

ELLE JAMES

TWISTED PAGE INC

Copyright © 2025 by Elle James

All rights reserved.

No part of this book may be reproduced in any form or by any electronic or mechanical means, including information storage and retrieval systems, without written permission from the author, except for the use of brief quotations in a book review.

Without in any way limiting the author's [and publisher's] exclusive rights under copyright, any use of this publication to "train" generative artificial intelligence (AI) technologies to generate text is expressly prohibited. The author reserves all rights to license uses of this work for generative AI training and development of machine learning language models.

ISBN EBOOK: 978-1-62695-530-1

ISBN PRINT: 978-1-62695-531-8

ISBN HARDCOVER: 978-1-62695-608-7

Dedicated to my readers who make my dreams come true by keeping me in the business I love dearly...WRITING! I love you all so much. Thank you for buying my books!
Elle James

AUTHOR'S NOTE

Enjoy other military books by Elle James

Bayou Brotherhood Protectors
Remy (#1)
Gerard (#2)
Lucas (#3)
Beau (#4)
Rafael (#5)
Valentin (#6)
Landry (#7)
Simon (#8)
Maurice (#9)

Visit ellejames.com for more titles and release dates
Join her newsletter at
https://ellejames.com/contact/

SIMON

BAYOU BROTHERHOOD PROTECTORS
BOOK # 8

New York Times & USA Today
Bestselling Author

ELLE JAMES

CHAPTER 1

"It's been a week and a half since Landry and Camille's wedding, and Gisele hasn't stopped talking about her cousin Holly." Rafael Romero held the end of the jon boat steady.

Sinclaire Simon Savier, who preferred to go by Simon, not his callsign Sin, raised the face shield on his welder's mask and lowered his torch. "Has Ms. Hazard had any more messages since her return to Bayou Mambaloa?"

Rafael shook his head. "Not so far. But then she's only been back a short time. Whoever left the message on her mirror in Atlanta might not know she left."

"Anyone who went to the trouble of writing a message on her mirror in her locked apartment most likely knows her every move." Simon set the torch on the ground and pulled the hood over his head. "Where's she staying?"

"She was staying at her grandmother's place," Rafael said. "It's on an island in the bayou."

Simon frowned. "Doesn't that limit her ability to get a job?"

"Not if you have access to a jon boat or a pirogue. I doubt anyone would try anything as long as she's with Bayou Mambaloa's Voodoo Queen."

"If they believe in that garbage."

Rafael cocked an eyebrow. "You don't believe in Voodoo?"

"No." Simon turned away and set the welder's hood on the worktable behind him.

"Don't you believe in magic?" Rafael asked.

"No." He'd learned that magic didn't exist. Luck didn't exist. What happened did so without the help of magic, curses or potions. He found it ridiculous and backward that so many people on the bayou believed in Voodoo.

Voodoo curses, gris-gris pouches and lucky rabbit's feet didn't affect the outcome of events.

His hand went to his pocket to feel the soft fur of Johnny Smallwood's lucky rabbit's foot. Memories flooded into Simon's mind.

Bang!

Simon dropped to the dirt, his heart slamming hard against his chest, his ears ringing. Dust spread in a wave like fog, clouding his vision, filling his nostrils and choking his lungs.

"Sin? Johnny? Ringer? Mack? Talk to me," La Blanc sounded in Simon's ear as if from the end of a very long tunnel.

"Sin here," Simon said, his own voice muffled in his numbed senses.

"Mack here," his other teammate reported in.

"I can't find Ringer," La Blanc said, his voice tight, desperate. "Oh, Jesus." Silence then, "I have Ringer. He's hit. Hey, man, hang in there. We'll get you out of here."

Simon's heart swelled into his throat at the hollow fear in La Banc's tone. Ringer was La Blanc's friend, his battle buddy. Like Johnny was Simon's. They were all friends, teammates, members of Delta Force. They'd trained, fought and spent most of their lives together. They had each other's backs.

"Johnny?" Simon choked out. "You hear me?" When his battle buddy didn't respond, Simon crawled through the chunks of broken brick, searching for his friend, "Johnny!"

His hand touched something softer than the rubble of the destroyed building. A groan sounded, and a hand reached out in the haze to grasp his arm in a desperate, almost painful grip.

"Johnny. That you, buddy?" Simon coughed the dust from his throat and knelt in the rubble. "Talk to me, man. Are you hit?"

His friend's hand squeezed his arm.

In the darkness, mired in the heavy dust filling the air,

Simon ran his free hand over his teammate, searching for a wound. When his fingers skimmed across Johnny's midsection, he encountered something warm and wet. A least one source of his friend's injury. He yanked off the olive-drab scarf he'd wrapped around his neck and pressed it into the bloody mess, applying pressure to slow the flow. "Stay with me, Johnny."

"Not going...any...where," Johnny croaked and gave a brief gurgling cough. "Dude," he wheezed, "do me...a ...favor."

"Anything," Simon said. "You got it."

"In my pocket."

Simon leaned close to hear Johnny's words, the ringing in his own ears making it difficult.

"What's in your pocket?" Simon asked. "And don't tell me it's a banana," he tried to joke, but the laughter wasn't in him.

"Ha," Johnny coughed. "Take it."

"Take what?"

"Get it," he said and coughed again.

Simon patted Johnny's pants pocket on the left and didn't feel anything. He did the same on the right pocket. Something was in there. Shoving his hand into the pocket, something soft brushed against his fingertip. In that moment, he knew what it was. He closed his hand around it and pulled it free.

The hand Johnny had on his arm slid down to where Simon held Johnny's lucky rabbit's foot. The idiot had carried it everywhere since he'd joined the Army.

"Keep it," Johnny said. "It's lucky."

Simon shook his head, glad the darkness kept his friend from seeing the movement. How could his rabbit's foot be lucky when it had allowed Johnny to be hit? The man was losing blood faster than Simon could staunch the flow.

"Yours now," Johnny's voice faded off. He drew in a rattling breath and let it out.

"Johnny, you need to keep it. It's your lucky charm," Simon said, pushing air past the knot in his throat.

Johnny's fingers wrapped around Simon's and the rabbit's foot. "You need it...more," he wheezed in a breath and let it out. "Lucky in battle." His fingers tightened. "Lucky in...love."

Though Simon could argue the luck in battle, he couldn't argue Johnny's luck in love. The man had found a woman strong enough to handle his many absences whenever he was deployed. A woman who'd stayed loyal and true to their love and union. A woman who'd given him a son, managed their home and worked a fulltime job, never complaining that he wasn't there every step of the way. She loved him, and he loved her with all his heart.

Johnny's body tensed, his hand on Simon's tightening. "Keep it," he said, his voice barely more than a raspy whisper.

"I'll give it to Lacy," Simon offered.

"No." Johnny's fingers tightened on Simon's. "Yours... Keep..."

"Okay," Simon said. "I'll keep it."

"Promise," Johnny whispered, the sound swirling with the dust still floating in the air.

"I promise." Simon maintained pressure on the wound with one hand while holding the rabbit's foot in the other.

Several seconds ticked by. The silence was deafening.

"Johnny?" Simon's fist curled around the lucky rabbit's foot, his chest tightening painfully. "Don't you leave me. You're my wingman. I need you. Lacy and Tyler need you."

"Tell Lacy...love her... love Ty..." Johnny's voice faded with each word. His hand loosened and slipped off Simon's.

Simon leaned close to his friend. "Johnny, stay with me, buddy." This couldn't be happening. They should be on their way back to their pickup point.

Fuck. He was losing his best friend.

Simon shook with the force of his emotions. He shook so violently he thought the explosion might have set off an earthquake.

"Simon?" A voice called to him as if from far away. A hand rested on his shoulder and shook him. "Hey, man, are you okay?"

Simon blinked his eyes open. Bright light surrounded him, not the dark haze of that Syrian night. Instead of being surrounded by rubble and choked by dust, he knelt on clean concrete, with bright sheets of aluminum stacked nearby.

The hand on his shoulder gently shook him again. "Simon, are you with me now?"

He looked into Rafael Romero's dark brown eyes.

His brows formed a wedge over his nose as his gaze locked with Simon's. "There you are." His lips twisted in a wry grimace. "For a moment there, I thought I'd somehow hurt you when I lost my grip on the hull." His frown eased.

Simon pinched the bridge of his nose, finding it difficult to pull himself out of Syria and back to...

"What...happened?" he asked.

"I dropped the hull of the boat we were working on. You'd have thought a bomb went off, the amount of noise it made." The frown returned. "Is that it? Did the noise trigger you?"

Simon pushed the images, emotions and that sense of loss to the back of his mind, behind the wall he'd worked so hard to erect between the past and present. "I'm fine," he said, his tone more abrupt than he'd intended.

Rafael held out a hand.

Simon took it reluctantly and let his teammate pull him to his feet.

"You were back in Syria, weren't you?"

"No, I just lost my balance," Simon lied.

Rafael laid an arm across his shoulder. "PTSD is real and nothing to be ashamed of. I still drop to the ground when I hear loud and unexpected noises. I still have nightmares about some of the hairier missions. I think we all do."

Simon shrugged and stepped away, forcing Rafael's arm to fall to his side. "I'm used to the nightmares," he admitted. "It's been a while since I've had one in the daytime."

"That's on me," Rafael said. "Wouldn't have happened if I hadn't dropped the hull."

Footsteps scraped on the concrete floor and echoed throughout the cavernous area of the old boat factory that the Bayou Brotherhood Protectors had remodeled into their regional headquarters.

Remy Montagne, the leader of their band of brothers, stopped next to the jon boat hull they had been working on minutes before and nodded. "It's looking good. Your welding has improved a lot since we reopened this place."

Still wobbling internally, Simon gave a brief nod and muttered, "Thanks."

Remy looked up from the boat at the two men. His brow furrowed briefly. "Something wrong?"

Simon shook his head. "No," he answered, hoping Rafael wouldn't tell the boss otherwise.

"Just finishing up," Rafael said.

"When you reach a stopping point, join us at the Crawdad Hole. I have some protector work to assign."

"Great." Rafael bent to retrieve the welder's mask from the floor. "We'll be right behind you."

Remy nodded. "See you there. Shelby gave me a pass for a couple of hours, but I'm not staying long. She's had the day off and could use a break from chasing Jean-Luc around all day."

"I can only imagine," Rafael said. "He's a very busy little guy."

"That boy learned to run before he learned to walk," Remy said. "Hell, I'm not sure he knows how to walk. He's going ninety miles an hour from dawn to dusk. He's a handful all right."

"I don't think I've seen a happier kid," Rafael noted. "Every time I see him, he's always up for a hug."

Remy chuckled. "He is, isn't he?"

Simon nodded, remembering that he hadn't checked in with Lacy and Ty in a week. He grabbed the torch from where he'd placed it on the floor. "I'll see you two shortly. I want to put this away and wash up."

"Sounds good," Remy said. "I'm out of here." He turned and walked away.

Simon wished Rafael would walk away as well. "You don't have to wait on me."

Rafael hesitated. "You could ride with me. That way, I'll be your designated driver."

"I won't need a designated driver," Simon said.

"So, I'll see you there in a few?" Rafael hadn't moved from where he stood.

"Don't worry about me," Simon said. "I'll be there. I just want to check on a friend."

"Okay, then. I'll see you there. I'm going to make a detour and pick up Gisele. Valentin said Ouida Mae will be there. They're bringing Ouida Mae's school principal out for a little bit of a girls' night out and hoping to include Gisele's cousin, Holly, when she gets off her shift waiting tables."

"Should be quite the crowd." Simon gave Rafael a mock salute. "See y'all there." He took the welder's mask from Rafael and headed for the storage cabinet, hoping to end the conversation.

After stowing the items, he found himself alone in the factory. In the bathroom, he splashed water on his face, trying to remove the memory of the Syrian dust and bring himself more firmly back to the present.

A quick glance at his reflection in the mirror confirmed he was the same physically as he'd been that morning getting ready for work. Inside, he didn't feel the same.

Whenever he had a flashback to that night in Syria, he came out of it shaken and emotionally wrecked. Much like he'd been when he'd carried his friend's body to the helicopter. For the next few hours, sometimes days, he walked around like a zombie, going through the motions, but not really engaging.

Thoughts of Johnny always made him think of the wife and son he'd left behind. It had been four years since Johnny had died.

Lacy had been heartbroken but refused to let her grief impact her son. She'd put on a brave face and kept moving. Kept loving her son. Kept working.

Because she hadn't let herself wallow, she'd been blessed with the opportunity to move on. She'd met a very nice man at her son's peewee baseball league. Though she was taking it slowly, she held onto hope for a future with potential for love with a man who would be good to her and her son.

Simon pulled out his cell phone and called Lacy.

"Simon, it's good to hear from you," Lacy answered immediately.

"Hi, Lacy. How's Tyler?"

"Keeping me on my toes, as always," she answered. "We're getting ready to go to a minor league baseball game with Mark."

"That's great," he said, smiling at the thought of Lacy and Tyler enjoying time with the new man in their lives. "I'm glad you're getting out there."

"Yeah, me, too," she said softly. "Did you have another flashback?"

He could always count on Lacy to see through his casual calls. "I was thinking of Johnny."

"You know he wouldn't have wanted you to blame yourself for his death."

Simon nodded, though she couldn't see it. "I know."

"And he would've wanted you to get on with living a happy life, not living through that awful night, over and over."

"Yeah," he said.

"I'll always love Johnny," Lacy said. "How could I

not? I see him in Tyler every day. He's the spitting image of his father—in looks and his nonstop personality." Lacy laughed.

"You've learned to live without him," Simon said.

"Physically, yes. But I've learned to live *with* him in my heart. I never even thought of loving another man, but Mark's growing on me." She sighed. "He's kind and gentle. He's good with Tyler, and he doesn't expect me to stop loving Johnny. He's willing to wait until I figure out whether there's room in my heart for him."

"He's a lucky man, Lacy. I'm glad you've found someone."

"Me, too. Life can be lonely without someone to share it with. I was lucky to have Johnny for as long as I did. Now, I'm lucky Mark and I have found each other."

Simon's heart swelled. He was happy for Lacy. Truly happy. "I just wanted to make sure you and Tyler are doing okay."

"We are," Lacy said. "But what about you? How are things in the bayou? Do you like working for the Brotherhood Protectors? Still getting along with the team?"

Simon laughed. "I'm great. What can I say? I grew up around here, and I have a great team, all of whom have my back."

"Hmmm," Lacy dragged out the sound. "You grew up around there, but do you feel like you've come home? Please tell me you aren't still living in the boarding house."

He grimaced. "Okay, I won't tell you."

"Sinclaire Simon Sevier, you promised me that you'd start looking for a house and that you'd set down roots and make a home for yourself."

Guilt made his stomach sour. He had promised those things the last time they'd talked. Sure, he'd had the time, just not the drive or desire.

"Have you even contacted a real estate agent?" Lacy asked.

He could lie and say he had. "No."

"I'm going to call Remy and ask for references. Then I'm setting up an appointment for you right now."

"I can do that," he said. "You're on your way to a ball game."

She sighed. "Fine. I don't have time right now, but I will call Remy tomorrow and ask him if you've made an appointment with a realtor. So, don't blow me off this time. I have your boss on speed dial."

"Yes, ma'am." He chuckled. "Look, I don't want to keep you, and I'm meeting the team at the Crawdad Hole."

"Good. I'm glad you're getting out, as well. While you're out, find a pretty girl to dance with."

"I don't dance," he said.

"Then it's about time you learned," Lacy said. "Women like to dance. Learn how to do it. And find you a nice young lady to love. You deserve to be happy."

"Take care of yourself, Lacy, and give Tyler a hug from Uncle Simon."

"Will do," she said. "And Simon...?"

"Yeah, Lacy?"

"Do you still have Johnny's lucky rabbit's foot?"

Simon's hand slipped into his pocket to feel the soft fur of the rabbit's foot. "I do."

"Good. Keep it with you," Lacy said. "It'll bring you luck."

"What if I don't believe in luck?"

Lacy tsked. "More's the shame. Luck is like magic and love. You have to believe in it for it to happen to you. Johnny believed, and he found me."

He didn't remind her that Johnny had had his rabbit foot on him when he'd died. Where had that luck been when he'd needed it?

"Be open, Simon," Lacy said softly. "Believe."

Simon ended that call with Lacy's words echoing in his head, along with the residual daydream of Johnny insisting he keep the lucky rabbit's foot.

He'd kept his promise, but he didn't feel any luckier for it.

Believe...

CHAPTER 2

"What time are you off?" Gisele called out.

"Ten," Holly answered as she passed out drinks to the table filled with her cousin and her lady friends. "But maybe later, if this place stays as full as it is. I can't leave Danny to handle all this by herself."

"Ah, but we want you to join us. This is girls' night out."

Holly gave Gisele a crooked smile. "And I'd love to be a part of it, but I've been on this job for less than two weeks. As nice as Rene is, I can't expect him to let me take the night off when they need all the help they can get."

"Want me to encourage the guys to leave so there are fewer customers to serve?" Ouida Mae, the high school science teacher, asked. "I'm sure if I told Valentin we need to thin the herd, he'd go along with it and get his buddies to comply."

"A few less men would be nice, but that would cut into Rene's profits and my tips." Holly set a beer in front of Ouida Mae. "But thanks for the offer. Besides, this girls' night out was in honor of Principal Ashcraft. It's her fortieth birthday. She needs all the love."

Holly lifted her chin toward the pretty, older woman of the group, seated at the opposite end of the table.

Joyce wore a shiny tiara the women had insisted she wear to announce to all in the bar that it was her birthday. As a high school principal, a role that required her to be a pillar of the community, she seemed shy and a little embarrassed at all the attention.

Though she hadn't wanted to get Gisele's hopes up, Holly secretly hoped to join the ladies' fun night before long.

The band struck up a lively polka, and couples moved to the floor.

Holly hurried over to the guys Ouida Mae had offered to send home. Gisele had identified the group as the security organization that had set up shop at the old boat factory. What had she called them? Bayou Brotherhood Protectors? Among them was Gisele's husband, Rafael, and Ouida Mae's man, Valentin. She'd met most of them when she'd crashed Camille and Landry's wedding at the courthouse, in her desperate hunt for Gisele.

Holly gathered empty mugs and took orders from the men. As she worked her way around the table, Remy Montagne, their leader, caught her eye and motioned for her to come closer.

He gave her his order for a beer and then asked, "Have you had any more messages since coming home to Bayou Mambaloa?"

Her cheeks heated as his words drew the attention of all the men at the table. She shook her head. "No."

"I still think it wouldn't hurt to have one of my men shadow you until you find out who's targeting you." He tipped his chin toward the man on his right. "I have Simon on standby. Just say the word, and he's yours."

Her gaze shifted to the man Remy offered, and the heat intensified in her cheeks. The man was all smoldering good looks with his dark hair, ice-blue eyes and impossibly broad shoulders. All hers?

Butterflies fluttered low in her belly.

She had enough problems. Having a hot guy follow her around would only add to them. She was home in the bayou to put curses to rest, not to stir up brand-new ones.

"Thank you, but I'm okay for now."

"You have my number," Remy said. "If you feel at all threatened here in Bayou Mambaloa, call."

"I will. Now, if you'll excuse me, I'll get your drinks." One last look at the man who could be all hers had her scurrying away to the safety of the bar, where she emptied the tray and waited for Rene to fill the orders for more drinks.

A beefy arm slipped around her waist. "Holly Gautier," a man's voice said too close to her ear, "when did you get back in town?"

Holly sighed and pushed the arm away from her body. "Hey, Cody. Watch the hands. Are you seated at the bar?"

He nodded and slipped his arm around her again. "I am. How about taking a spin on the dance floor with me? You know, for old times' sake."

"Hands off, Cody." She shoved his arm away for the second time. "I'm working."

"Rene will let you have just one dance. Won't you, Rene?" Cody said to the bar owner.

Holly gave her boss an almost imperceptible shake of her head.

Rene frowned. "She's working, and we're short-handed. If you want a dance partner, find someone who isn't one of my staff."

Cody snorted. "I'm disappointed, Rene. I thought we were friends."

Rene grabbed a mug and placed it beneath the tap. "I don't know where you got that idea. Now, can I get you a drink? If not, I have plenty of other orders to fill." He pulled the lever, filled the mug and set it on Holly's tray. "That completes your order," he said. "A customer's waving for your attention. Best be gettin'."

Holly gave Rene a grateful smile, hefted the heavy tray and turned.

Cody's arm came out again, catching her across the belly, bringing her to a complete halt so fast she pitched forward. The drinks on her tray rocked precariously.

For a moment, she thought they'd settle. She was wrong. One mug tipped, knocking into the next. The domino effect sent the lot crashing to the floor, splashing beer and broken glasses in a six-foot radius.

"Goddamn, woman!" Cody jumped back. "You got beer all over my new boots." He stamped his feet, trying to shake off the liquid. When that didn't help, he held out his hand to Rene. "Give me a rag. Quick. Before it sets in."

Rene wadded up the damp rag he'd been using to wipe the bar and pitched it hard at Cody's face.

He didn't get his hands up in time to deflect it, and it slapped hard across his forehead.

Holly would have laughed, except she was covered in beer and surrounded by broken mugs and bottles.

The men at the Brotherhood Protectors' table sprang to their feet.

The one called Simon was there first, pushing Cody aside to get to her.

"Hey," Cody protested. "Watch it."

Simon ignored him, shuffled through the mess,

regardless of any damage it might cause his boots, and scooped Holly up in his arms.

She slung her arm around his neck, surprised and unprepared to be swept off her feet. "What are you doing?"

"Getting you to safety," he said.

"But I have to clean up the mess," she protested.

"It would be best to start from the outside and work your way in, rather than walking through broken glass," he pointed out as he set her on her feet at the perimeter of the disaster.

Rene came around the counter with a broom and a dustpan. Danny, the other waitress, rolled a mop bucket out from the back storeroom.

Much to Holly's chagrin and secret admiration, Simon and his team took over. Simon manned the broom, and Remy held the dustpan as he swept up the broken glass.

Ouida Mae's husband carried a large, plastic-lined trash bin and set it close by.

Within minutes, Simon and Remy had the glass cleared. Rafael mopped up the beer, and Valentin used several bar towels to dry the floor. In less than five minutes, the barroom floor was returned to order, cleaner than before the beer had been spilled.

Rene had a fresh tray of drinks waiting.

Meanwhile, Cody stood back, fussing over his new boots. "I'll send you the bill if my boots are ruined," he said to Rene.

Rene's eyes narrowed. "Holly, say the word and I'll file assault charges on Cody."

Cody's eyes widened. "Assault? That's bullshit."

Rene met Holly's gaze. "Did you want Cody to put his arm around you?"

Holly shook her head, her face burning. Every customer in the bar was focused on the entire altercation. "No."

"Did you, or did you not tell him to keep his hands off?" Rene's gaze went from Holly to Cody.

"I did tell him," Holly said.

"We're old friends," Cody blustered. "I put my arm around you as a friendly gesture, not assault."

Holly lifted the tray of drinks and gave Cody a hard stare. "We might've been friends in the past, but we aren't now. Don't touch me again, or I will file assault charges. Now, either get a drink or leave. I have work to do."

When Cody started toward her, Simon stepped between them and followed her to the table where his buddies had all reconvened.

She smiled at the men at the table and started handing out their drinks. "Thanks, guys. The drinks are on me."

"That's not necessary," Simon said as he helped distribute the mugs.

"I insist," she said. "You did my job. The least I can do is buy this round." She held up her hand. "Thanks for coming to my rescue." Before they could argue further, she grabbed her tray and hurried to the next table.

Once she had all her customers happy, she returned to the bar, her jeans still damp with beer.

"I think Danny and I can manage the rest of the evening if you'd like to join your friends," Rene said.

"I don't mind working—just not covered in beer."

Rene's lips twisted in a grimace. He wet a fresh bar towel and handed it across to her. "Sorry about Cody."

"Why should you be sorry?" she said as she used the damp towel to wash the sticky beer from her arms. "Cody was the asshole—and it's kind of part of the job, isn't it?"

"Not in my bar," Rene insisted. "I don't tolerate abusive customers."

"Thanks." She handed the towel back to Rene. "Well, he was half right. We used to be friends."

"What happened?"

"Holly, sweetie." Lissette, the cousin she tried to steer clear of, appeared at the bar. "I can't believe Cody was such a dick. But the hunky rescue was *ah-mazing*." She grinned. "Wow. Talk about a knight in shining armor, sweeping a girl off her feet. Have you been keeping secrets from your favorite cousin?"

Holly felt the blood rush from her face.

SECRETS KILL

That had been the message written on her bathroom mirror in Atlanta and was the reason she'd returned to Bayou Mambaloa. It was the continuation of the curse that had taken Paul and her parents from her.

Holly stared at her cousin. "Why would you say that?"

Lissette's eyes widened, and she blinked several times. "Say what?"

Holly studied her least favorite cousin. The one who had always gotten them in trouble as kids and had maintained the reputation of a troublemaker into adulthood. "Secrets. You said secrets."

"Oh, that." She waved a hand dismissively. "I was just talking about the secret you've been keeping about your relationship with that hottie." She shot a glance toward Simon. "How long has that been going on? You've barely been back. Was it love at first sight?"

Simon's gaze met Holly's. Heat flooded her cheeks as she remembered the warmth of his hands on her as he'd lifted her off the floor like she weighed nothing. She was no lightweight at five feet seven inches tall. She dragged her gaze away from his. "There's no secret."

"Then you're all out in the open about your new love toy."

"He's not my love toy."

"Lissette, are you bothering Holly while she's working?" Gisele appeared on the other side of Holly.

"Not at all," Lissette blinked innocently. "I heard

Rene tell her to take the rest of the night off. So, she's not working at all."

"Then let me rephrase my question," Gisele said. "Lissette, are you bothering Holly?"

Lissette's pretty brows drew together. "No. I just wanted to congratulate her on bagging one of the hot guys from your man's security team."

"I haven't bagged a man," Holly said.

Gisele glanced toward the door. "Isn't that Jonathon Reneau, of the mega-car-dealership Reneaus?"

Lissette's head spun toward the entrance. "Ohhh. It is."

"Didn't he just take over management of their family business?"

"He did," Lissette said breathlessly.

"I hear he's the state's most eligible bachelor," Gisele murmured.

Holly fought to keep a straight face as Lissette patted her perfectly arranged, long dark hair.

"Pardon me," Lissette said. "I need to talk to that man." She hurried across the room, slowing as she approached her target.

"I don't think there's a woman alive who loves men as much as Lissette." Gisele redirected her attention to Holly. "Was Lissette telling the truth? Has Rene given you the rest of the night off?"

Holly nodded. "Not that I'm in any condition to

join the party." She glanced down at her damp clothes that smelled of stale beer and whiskey.

Gisele smiled, slid the bag she carried off her shoulder and handed it to Holly. "I was in New Orleans today doing a little shopping and found the cutest outfit."

Holly shook her head. "There's no way I'd fit into it. I mean, I'm an Amazon next to you and Lizette. I take after my mother, not the petite Gautier women."

Gisele smiled. "You're taller, but you're slender, and I'll bet we have the same waist and hip measurements. It's a dress that comes down to my ankles. On you, it'll be shorter, but adorable. Try it."

"But I don't have shoes to match."

Gisele studied the ballet flats she'd worn for work. "They're perfect. The dress is casual, a little Bohemian and will go great with your auburn hair."

Out of reasons not to join their girls' night out, Holly accepted the bag. "I won't stay long. I need to get up early tomorrow to do laundry and clean my house."

"We'll take whatever time you're willing to give." Gisele turned her toward the bathrooms. "Go. We might need your help with matchmaking for the high school principal."

"I'm not a match—"

"Just go." Gisele gave her a gentle shove.

Holly snagged a clean bar towel and hurried to

the bathroom, not really in the mood to be social, but resigning herself to the night. Gisele had been there for her when she'd come blasting back into town after being gone for six months.

She'd helped her find a place to live—a place she never would've thought of. Rental property in the summertime was at a premium, but Gisele had friends with a houseboat they weren't using and had convinced them to rent it to Holly for cheap, with the promise of cleaning it and performing some minor maintenance.

She'd moved out of her grandmother's house and into the houseboat earlier that day. It was perfect for her budget, which was whatever she made working for Rene and the tips she brought home.

And it came with a pirogue she could use to paddle out to her grandmother, Madam Gautier's place in the bayou, not too far from town. Not that her grandmother had been available since she'd arrived. She'd been back and forth to New Orleans, stocking up on food and supplies for her business.

She'd promised to be available soon to help Holly work on finding the source of the curse that had followed her from Bayou Mambaloa to Atlanta.

Holly hoped to connect with her grandmother, who also happened to be the friendly neighborhood Voodoo Queen. She helped so many of the inhabitants of Bayou Mambaloa; surely, she could help her own granddaughter vanquish whatever curse was affecting her life before anyone else was hurt or killed.

In the bathroom, she stripped out of her damp clothes. She used the bar towel for a quick wipe down to remove the remaining beer and whiskey from her skin.

Then she removed the dress from the bag and pulled it over her head. The soft, flowy material floated down her body. Though loose, it molded to her curves, the hem reaching mid-calf. A smocked bodice stretched over her full breasts, and the little capped sleeves fit best worn off her shoulders, which meant if she didn't want to display bra straps. The bra had to go.

She unclasped it and pulled it off, then slid her arms back into the little sleeves.

A glance in the mirror made Holly smile.

This was a typical Gisele dress, light, airy and colorful. Not what Holly would choose, but Gisele had been right. The combination of gold, green and blue complemented her auburn hair and green eyes. With her height she'd gotten from her mother's side of the family, the dress length was perfect, exposing her trim calves.

The whole effect made her look less tired and more like a girl going to a party.

"All right then," she said to her reflection. The night was looking up.

She stuffed her damp clothing into the bag,

fluffed her hair and added a touch of lipstick. In a hurry to get back out to where her cousin and friends were, she flung open the door and charged out of the bathroom into the dimly lit hallway and promptly bumped into a wall of muscles.

Hands gripped her arms to steady her.

Holly looked up into the ice-blue eyes of the man who'd come to her rescue earlier. "Oh. It's you."

He nodded. "Yes, it is. Are you all right?"

"Of course," she said, suddenly conscious of how low the dress rested on the swell of her breasts. With little effort, the top could be tugged even lower to display all. Not that she'd do that in front of this man. Or that he'd be tempted to do it himself—and certainly not in public.

Her body heated as her thoughts spiraled.

"Excuse me," she said. "I have to go."

Before I spontaneously combust.

She turned to run.

His hand reached out to touch her arm. "You know, Remy's offer stands. I could shadow you for a while. I can help head off things like what happened tonight."

His fingers, though barely touching her skin, sent sparks throughout her body. Sparks that lit a fire deep in her core.

"Cody is an annoyance I can handle," she said. *I can't seem to handle what you're doing to me.* "I'm fine. So far, I haven't received any more messages. And I'm not sure what you could do that would help that problem anyway. My grandmother is the only one who has a shot at it."

Simon frowned. "Your grandmother is a bodyguard?"

Holly laughed. "No. Of course not. She's our resident Voodoo Queen, and possibly the only person who can break whatever curse is following me."

Simon stepped back, his eyebrows rising up his forehead. "Wait...what?"

"I'm cursed," she said, bracing herself for yet another Voodoo non-believer. "Every time something bad has happened, I find a message. Either written in the sand, on the bark of a tree or the latest...on my mirror in the bathroom of my apartment in Atlanta."

"And you think it's Voodoo?"

"Yes. More specifically, a Voodoo curse." She shook her head. "I can see you don't believe in magic. That's okay. I don't need you to. I'll work with my grandmother, Madam Gautier, to get through this. In the meantime, it's best to stay away from me. The curse seems to take people I care for most." She frowned, realizing what she'd just implicated. "Not that I care the most about you, but you never know...collateral damage and all."

Okay, now she was just blathering and sounding more and more idiotic. "I have to go." *Before I talk myself into another corner.*

She ducked her head and marched past Simon and out into the barroom where her friends were waiting.

"Oooo, look at you," Gisele said. "I knew you'd kill that dress."

"It's gorgeous," Ouida Mae seconded.

"And it brings out the green in your eyes," Joyce Ashcraft added.

"Thank you." Holly sank into the chair beside Gisele, glad to get off her feet if only for a few minutes. Hyper-aware of a certain man, her peripheral vision found him settling in at the table with the other members of his team, his gaze on the ladies at her table.

Yeah, fifteen minutes tops, and she was out of there. She didn't need a bodyguard. Not one who stirred her blood so thoroughly. The last thing she needed was to get involved with someone. Her curse might be his death sentence. She refused to let that happen.

"Are you sure you should be seen with me?" she whispered to Gisele. "It might've been better if I'd stayed in Atlanta. I don't want any more of my family or friends to die because I was selfish and came back home."

Gisele laid her hand over Holly's. "Don't borrow trouble. Besides, I'm not convinced you're cursed."

Holly stared at her cousin. "I would've expected you, of all people, to be more open to the possibility."

"Normally, I am," Gisele said. "It's just that your situation seems different. I'm not getting a magic vibe."

"The message on my mirror appeared only when I had a hot shower, and it steamed the glass. It disappeared when the steam dried."

"That could be explained," Gisele said.

"My apartment door was locked. There was no sign of forced entry."

"The perp is good at picking locks." Gisele smiled. "What else ya got?"

"The messages I found in the sand near my folks' boathouse. There were no footprints around it."

"That can be explained as well," Gisele said. "They could have dragged a branch across the sand to hide them. But stop worrying about that for now. We have a job to do." She leaned close. "Joyce is our high school principal; it's her birthday, and she hasn't been laid since her divorce six years ago."

"What are we supposed to do about that? Pay some man to take her to bed?" Holly studied Joyce as she tapped her toe to the beat of the music, her gaze on the couples dancing. The woman was oblivious to her friends' proposed machinations, which was just as well.

Holly would have hated the idea of her cousin and friends setting her up with a male prostitute.

"No, no, no." Gisele shook her head. "She needs a little romance in her life. There has to be an available man who'll treat her right. Someone who isn't intimidated by a powerful, take-charge woman."

"Don't look now, but a man just stopped beside her," Holly murmured.

The man in question swayed a little as he held out his hand. "Care to dance?"

Joyce shot a wary glance toward the ladies at the table.

Gisele nodded, encouragingly.

Holly shrugged.

Ouida Mae grinned. "Don't worry about us. We'll be here when you get back."

Joyce gave the man a weak smile and allowed him to help her to her feet. Soon, they were two-stepping around the dance floor.

Well, Joyce was two-stepping, while her partner was stepping on her toes and stumbling. After several passes, the man's movements only got worse.

Holly cringed. "Think we should rescue her?"

"Yeah." Gisele rose from her chair. "If we don't do it soon, she'll be black and blue all over."

The three women had just started across the floor when Joyce's dance partner tripped and face-planted on the floor.

Simon and Landry rushed forward, lifted the man by the arms and half-carried him to the exit.

Rene met the men at the door and held it open so they could carry the man out.

While her dance partner was being handled, Joyce

stood in the middle of the dance floor, her eyes wide, shaking her head.

Before her friends could reach her, the band started playing again.

A man stepped up to Joyce and offered his hand.

Gisele grabbed Holly and Ouida Mae, stopping them before they stepped out onto the dance floor. "Wait."

"Is that Mitchell Marceau?" Ouida Mae whispered.

Gisele nodded. "I almost didn't recognize him. He's usually wearing an old T-shirt covered in worm dirt or fish guts from working all day at the marina."

"Dang, he cleans up well," Ouida Mae said.

"Let's see if he's got two left feet," Holly suggested. "We might still need to rescue Joyce."

They stood back, watching as Mitch led Joyce around the dance floor, his footwork simple but smooth, all the while talking and smiling at the pretty principal.

"Well, I'll be gobsmacked," Gisele said. "I would never have guessed Marceau could dance so well."

"Me either but look at him go like it's as easy as breathing." Ouida Mae smiled. "It's nice to see Principal Ashcraft having a good time."

"I think we can take our seats," Holly said. "She seems to be in good hands."

As they started toward their table, Holly caught sight of Cody making his way toward her. "Oh, great," she muttered beneath her breath, ducked her head and pretended she didn't see him.

"Glad to see Rene let you off early. We can have that dance now." He held out his hand.

"Sorry," a deep voice said from behind Holly. "She's already spoken for." Simon stepped up beside her, took her hand and led her past Cody onto the wooden floor sprinkled with sawdust.

Holly cast a glance over her shoulder.

Cody's eyebrows formed a deep V on his forehead as he glared at Simon's back.

Already back at their table, Ouida Mae and Gisele each gave her a thumbs up while grinning from ear to ear.

"You don't have to go through with the dance," she said as he swung her into his arms.

He paused and raised an eyebrow.

Her gaze shot to Cody, standing at the edge of the dance floor. "Well, maybe it would be a good thing to go a few times around." She lifted her chin toward the disgruntled man. "Cody's lurking."

"You might change your mind after I've stepped on your toes."

"I'm sure it would be a lot less painful than being manhandled by Cody."

Simon led her expertly, keeping time to the music and even twirling her out and back like a seasoned professional.

When the music came to a stop, Holly laughed up

at him, breathless and flushed. "You undersold your abilities. Where did you learn to dance?"

He didn't move to take her back to the table, but kept her in his arms, holding her hand loosely, his other hand still at the small of her back. "My mother and father loved to dance. They took me with them on numerous occasions. My mother insisted I learn to dance, saying women love a man who can dance."

"She's right." Holly tilted her head, studying the man. "And yet you joined the military…?"

He nodded. "We have a long line of military in my family. My great-grandfather, grandfather, grandmother, mother, father, my brother and me."

"Wow. That's some lineage."

"We might be a military family, but we also know how to have fun."

"Thank you all for your service." She glanced toward her friends. "I guess I should rejoin my friends."

Simon's hand at the small of her back pulled her a little closer. "Cody's coming. I can take you back to the table, or we can move right into the next dance."

She caught sight of Cody making a beeline toward them. "Next dance, please."

The music started, and Simon swept her away from the oncoming Cody, moving smoothly in a lilting waltz.

It had been a long time since Holly had danced,

but with Simon leading, she was able to follow with ease.

Simon glanced down at her. "So, what's Cody's deal that he thinks he has a shot with you, when he clearly doesn't?"

"In high school, Paul, Cody and I were a little friend group. We went everywhere together. After high school, I went off to college to follow in my parents' footsteps and earned a degree in biology. When I returned home, our little trio fell back in place until Paul asked me to be his girlfriend. Cody lost his shit. He was sure I'd choose him." She snorted. "I told him I never felt anything other than friendship for him, but he wouldn't let it go."

"Is that why you left Bayou Mambaloa?"

She shook her head, her brow furrowing. "No. I left because of the curse you don't believe in."

"Tell me about it. Maybe you'll convince me to believe."

She drew in a breath, still moving about the floor to the three-count beat of the waltz. "My folks worked as biologists for the state to help preserve the bayou ecosystem. I worked in a lab, studying samples brought in from different locations around industries on the edges of the bayou."

When she paused, he swung her out and back, giving her a moment to think of the words that wouldn't sound crazy to a man who didn't believe in Voodoo or magic.

"One day, I found a message burned into the bark of a cypress tree near the home where I lived with my parents. It said, in all caps, SECRETS KILL."

"Messages don't just burn into tree bark by themselves," he said softly. "People make those happen."

"Whatever." She shrugged. "That night, my boyfriend, Paul, drove into the bayou and drowned. They inspected his car. Nothing was wrong with it. The brakes were functional. It was a clear night. There were no skid marks on the road to indicate he'd dodged an animal or was forced off the road by another driver. He just ended up in the bayou. When they found him, he was still in his seatbelt. No sign of struggle to free himself or try to get out of the vehicle. The Medical Examiner didn't find any sign of head trauma that would've knocked him out."

"Could it have been suicide?" Simon asked.

She drew a deep breath and shook her head. "Paul wasn't the kind of guy who would take his own life. He had a good job and made a good living. He'd just purchased a house and was scheduled to move in a week from that day."

"And he had a great girlfriend." Simon stared down into her eyes. "Doesn't make sense."

"The curse," Holly concluded. "A week later, I found another message drawn in the sand near my parents' boat dock." She remembered that day so clearly.

"What was the message?" Simon asked.

"The same one on my mirror in Atlanta and the tree at my parents' house—SECRETS KILL."

"Again, that sounds more like something written by a person, not a curse."

"That's what Gisele says. I found that message the morning my parents went boating and never came back."

She stumbled a bit. Simon helped her regain her footing. "Are you okay?"

She nodded. "Their boat was found. It had capsized out in the Gulf. No bodies. Since the people I cared about most were gone and their only connection was to me, I knew I was cursed. I was afraid to stay in Bayou Mambaloa. I thought about my grandmother, cousins and friends. I couldn't stay and risk the curse taking them from me. So, I left and moved to Atlanta, hoping that it was far enough away the curse wouldn't continue to take more of the people I cared about. After six months, the official report on my parents' accident was issued. It said they were missing, presumed dead."

Simon stopped dancing in the middle of the floor. "I'm sorry."

She looked up into his eyes. "It's been six months, and nothing has turned up. No bones. Nothing."

"Then you found the message in the mirror in Atlanta," he said.

She nodded. "I had to come back. To warn my

family members and friends. I don't know who the curse will target next."

"Have you thought that maybe you'll be the next target?"

"I have." Her eyes narrowed. "If I can't figure out a way to vanquish the curse. I pray it comes for me. Not anyone else. Then, if I can't fight back…if I die… maybe the curse will end with me."

CHAPTER 3

SIMON STARED down into Holly's moss-green irises, her pain evident in the dark circles beneath her eyes.

"You might believe in curses," he said, "but I think the curse is someone targeting you and your family. I also think you need the protection you've rejected. Let me help you find the answers. Let me protect you from whoever is doing this."

She leaned her forehead against his chest, her arms encircling his waist. "If only that's all it took. My grandmother is busy ministering to the entire community. I've been waiting for her to free up some time for me. Once she does, I'm sure she'll be able to help." She leaned back and looked up into his eyes. "But thanks for the offer. I think I'll be okay until then."

"Like your folks and your boyfriend? You only had a couple of hours' notice. It's been what, a week and a half since your last message? Are you sure you can wait for your grandmother?"

"I'll make do," she murmured. "Mémère usually knows how to handle situations, curse or no curse." She gave Simon a weak grin and headed for her table of friends.

Gisele patted the seat beside her. "Sit. Spill. We want all the details while we wait for Mitchell to let Joyce off the dance floor."

Still standing, Holly glanced over her shoulder at the pair laughing and kicking up their heels to a lively Cotton-eyed Joe. They looked adorable, and she was happy for them.

Her gaze slipped to Simon as he rejoined his buddies at their table. "I'm going to call it a night," Holly said.

Gisele's eyes widened. "You can't do that and leave us hanging."

"We want to know all about that dance with the handsome Simon," Ouida Mae insisted.

Holly gave them a twisted smile. "It was nice. He's a good guy, and his mother made sure he learned how to dance."

"Props to his mom," Gisele said. "You two looked like you belonged together."

Holly frowned. "Oh, please, don't go there. Save your matchmaking for the nice principal. Until I get to the bottom of the curse, I'm not looking for a relationship."

Gisele touched Holly's arm. "Oh, sweetie. Is that it? Are you worried that whoever you love will be affected by the curse?"

Holly sighed. "Precisely. And I'm worried about you, Mémère, my friends—everyone I care about." She looked from Gisele to Ouida Mae and back. "Please, promise me you'll be careful. I don't know who the curse will target next."

Gisele rose from her seat and hugged her cousin. "You be careful. And consider letting someone provide your protection until we figure this out."

"I'll think about it," Holly said. "Now, I'm headed to the houseboat. I haven't even had a chance to put sheets on the bed."

Gisele nodded toward the table of men. "At the very least, let one of the guys follow you there and make sure you get there safely."

Holly shook her head. "No need. I'll be okay and extra careful. Thanks for inviting me to your girls' night out. Maybe I'll be more in a party mood for the next one."

"You've been on your feet all evening. It's hard to party when you're tired," Ouida Mae said. "Normally, I'm the one exhausted after teaching all day. But it's summer vacay, and I'm free for a few more weeks. Valentin and I are going to New Orleans next weekend. We're taking the kids to the aquarium." She smiled across at her husband and wiggled her fingers in a little wave.

Holly envied her friends' happiness and prayed the curse didn't go after them. They'd gone through a lot to get to their current happy state.

"Everything's going to be all right, soon enough." Gisele gave Holly another hug. "I'll nudge Mémère and see if she can get free up to help you. She's been super busy lately with sick neighbors."

"I understand. I'm just worried that the longer we wait, the more likely someone else will be hurt or killed. There's bad juju. I left Bayou Mambaloa, hoping the curse would leave with me, that all of you would be safe. It seemed to have worked for six months. Why has it returned? Why now?"

"We'll get to the bottom of it," Gisele said. "Love you, cuz."

"Love you, too," Holly said. "I'll clean the dress and get it back to you soon."

"No way," Gisele said. "It's yours now. It looks so much better on you, and like Joyce said, it brings out the green in your eyes. Go, now. Get some rest." She turned Holly toward the exit and gave her a little push.

Her heart full of familial love yet weighed down by the thought of losing any one of them, Holly left the Crawdad Hole and stepped out into the lingering heat and humidity of a bayou summer night.

She drew in a deep breath and walked out to where she'd parked her car. A big truck blocked her view of her little car. When she rounded the tall hood, she came to a halt.

Cody West leaned against the driver's side of her car, arms folded over his chest, one boot crossed over the other.

Her back stiffened. "Cody, please move. I'm tired and just want to go home."

He didn't move. "I didn't like the way that Simon dude was acting like you belonged to him." He straightened and waved toward her and back to himself. "You and me...we go way back. We were inseparable as kids and teens."

"That's right. You, me and Paul hung out. As friends."

"Until Paul moved in on you." His brow dipped low. "He knew how I felt about you, and still, he moved in first."

Holly held up a hand. "Cody, you were always my friend. Nothing more."

"How do you know it's nothing more?" Before Holly could react, Cody grabbed her and yanked her against his chest. "We've never kissed."

Holly pressed her hands to his chest and pushed hard. "There's a reason we never kissed," she said through gritted teeth, turning her head to avoid the man's mouth descending toward hers. "I'm not interested, Cody."

His breath hot on her cheek, he said, "You won't

kiss me, someone you've known all your life, but you're panting after a stranger?"

"Let go of me," Holly said, "or I'll scream."

"Go ahead," he said. "No one will hear over the music."

Holly stomped on Cody's foot, her ballet flats making no impression. With her arms trapped to her sides and too close to knee him in the groin, she had to stop him before his lips claimed hers.

Leaning her head back, she snapped it forward. Her forehead slammed into his nose.

"Goddammit, Holly!" Cody yelled and let go of one of her arms to clutch his nose, blood streaming down his chin. "You broke my nose!"

"Be glad she did it, because I would've done a lot worse," a voice said from behind Holly.

She glanced over her shoulder at Simon.

His jaw tight, his eyes narrowed to slits, he glared at Cody. "Get your hand off her."

Cody swept his hand across his bloody nose. "Get lost," he said, his other hand squeezing Holly's arm to the point it would leave bruises. "We were having a private discussion."

"The hell we were," Holly said.

Cody sneered. "You barely know her. I've known her all my life. What's it to you anyway?"

"Let go of me, Cody," Holly said.

"You and I are meant to be together," Cody said.

Holly shook her head. "The truth is, we'll never be together because—"

"Because she's my girl," Simon said and karate-chopped Cody's arm, breaking his grip on Holly.

She stepped backward until she leaned into Simon.

"You've got to be kidding." Cody rubbed his arm. "She's been back for a little more than a week." He turned to Holly. "You can't possibly be his girl."

Tired of the fight and ready to be in her own place with her feet up, Holly lifted her chin, slid her hand into Simon's and said, "You're right, it's only been a short time, and we haven't made any announcements because it's all so new between us. But, yes, we're...together." She raised the hand holding his, if a bit awkwardly, and let it fall to her side.

Cody rubbed his arm where Simon had chopped him, his eyes narrow, his gaze going back and forth between Simon and Holly.

"That's right," Simon said. "And if you ever try to hurt her again, you'll answer to me."

Cody snorted. "I'm not afraid of you."

"No?" another voice said behind them. "Then you might consider that he comes with backup."

Holly glanced over her shoulder to find Remy and the rest of Simon's team forming a semi-circle around them. Her heart swelled at the support.

Simon's hand squeezed hers gently. He raised it

and pressed his lips to her knuckles. "Ready to go home, darlin'?"

Her pulse fluttered at the endearment, even though she knew it was all for show. "I am."

Simon cocked an eyebrow at Cody. "You can leave now."

Cody lifted his chin in defiance, then directed a sneer toward Holly. "You were meant for me, not this poser. You'll be mine."

"Never," she said. "You're delusional. Even if Paul hadn't been in the picture, I wouldn't have chosen you if you were the last man on earth."

The semi-circle of men moved closer.

Cody shook his head. "I'm leaving, but not because of you losers." He sidestepped Simon, climbed into his truck and revved the engine. When he shifted into gear, he hit the accelerator, spitting up gravel from his back tires. The truck lurched forward, narrowly missing Remy.

Remy stood his ground without flinching.

Cody and his monster truck left the parking lot, tires squealing as they spun on pavement, carrying the man and his attitude away.

Once Cody's vehicle disappeared out of sight, Holly's shoulders sagged. She let go of Simon's hand, shoved her fingers through her hair and looked up into Simon's blue eyes. "Thanks. I was running out of ways to convince him to let me go."

His lips quirked on the corners. "You were doing

a decent job of it, based on the amount of blood on his shirt."

She turned to the others. "And thank you all for showing up when you did. I would've felt bad if Simon and Cody had gotten into a fist fight."

"I wouldn't have felt bad." Simon clenched his fists. "The guy needs to be taught a lesson on how to respect a woman."

"Now that the show's over, I'm going to head home. Thanks again." She waved a hand, unlocked her car and got in. As soon as she started the engine, the air conditioner blasted out cool air, causing condensation to form on the outside of the windshield.

Fully aware of Simon standing beside the car, it took a moment for Holly to realize the condensation wasn't filling in all the way across the glass. Slowly, words appeared, making Holly's blood grow cold. Though she was looking at them in reverse, the message was clear.

SECRETS KILL

Holly pushed the door open and scrambled out of the car. She tripped over the hem of the dress and pitched forward into Simon's arms.

He caught her and held her against his chest until she got her feet firmly beneath her. "What's wrong?"

She leaned into him, turning sideways to point at her car. "That." Her hand shook. "The windshield."

Simon moved forward with a protective arm

around her, circling the front of the car. His team closed in around them as they stared at the message framed by the condensation.

"Secrets kill," Remy said softly. "The same message as the one on the mirror in your Atlanta apartment?"

She nodded. "Yes. The same that appeared on the tree before Paul died and the sandy beach when my parents' boat capsized six months ago." She trembled. "The first two messages were followed immediately by death and loss. I have to admit...I'm afraid."

"There's no shame in that," Simon said. "It's a threat."

"If it's not a direct threat to me," she said, "I'm afraid of who will die next."

"You say the first two messages were in the sand and on a tree?" Remy asked.

Holly nodded. "Yes. In the sand where my parents lived and on a tree outside my boyfriend's house."

Simon and Remy exchanged a glance. "Sounds like they were targeted specifically."

"The last two messages were in your apartment and on your vehicle."

Holly drew in a breath and let it out. "So, it's me." She let the breath out. "Thank goodness. At least it's not someone else."

Remy shook his head. "You need protection."

Holly's gaze went to the car and the message

carved out of the condensation. She'd always valued her independence. Her parents had spent so much time away from home pursuing various scientific endeavors that she'd learned to be on her own. However, independence was one thing; staying alive was another.

Holly squared her shoulders. "What does protection entail?"

Remy smiled and then schooled his face. "You need someone with you twenty-four-seven."

"Wait." She shook her head. "Every minute of the day?"

Remy nodded. "It does you no good if you send him home at the end of the day. If someone targets you, they're watching you, waiting to catch you when you least expect it...when you're alone and vulnerable."

"I've been alone a lot since I've been back," she noted. "Why hasn't it happened by now?"

"It might be a scare tactic," Simon explained.

Valentin stepped forward. "Like psychological warfare. Keeps you guessing until bam!" He smacked his fist into his palm.

Holly jerked back.

Simon's hand came up to rest at the small of her back.

She didn't want to admit it, but his warmth and strength were reassuring.

"Does that mean whoever provides that protection will be living with me until whatever this is stops?"

Remy nodded. "He'll guard you day and night."

"I have a job. I can't have someone hanging around while I work."

Remy's lips twisted into a wry grin. "I'm sure Rene at the Crawdad Hole won't mind. It would be like having an extra bouncer he wouldn't have to pay."

"I'm not a celebrity," Holly argued. "I can't afford a twelve-hour bodyguard, much less one who's with me twenty-four-seven."

"Brotherhood Protectors provide protection to those who need it, no matter their ability to pay for our services. Our founder, Hank Patterson, and his wife, Sadie McClain, set up a foundation to fund the work we do. All you have to do is accept our services, and we do the rest."

"I really don't want to announce to everyone that I'm scared and had to hire a bodyguard." Was she really considering accepting their help? "Could we keep it on the down low?"

Simon coughed. "It makes sense to keep up the tale we fed your friend Cody."

Holly rubbed the arm that still hurt from where he'd squeezed it so hard. "He's not my friend."

"Your former friend," Simon corrected. "He

doesn't seem the type to give up easily, and I think you broke his nose."

"He might come after me again," Holly agreed. "So, you're saying we should pretend that you and I are together, at least while I try to figure out what's going on...?"

Simon nodded. "Unless you want someone else to take the assignment."

Holly's pulse fluttered again at the thought of being with Simon every minute of every day. He was a lot to take in. "It's not like our relationship is real." She could keep emotions out of it, especially if they were wrong and the curse wasn't targeting her but the people she cared about. All she had to do was keep from caring too much for the guy. She could do that. She barely knew him. And she wouldn't wish her affection on anyone the curse could target all because she was weak and allowed herself to actually...you know...fall in love.

Another glance at the message on the windshield helped her make her decision. "Okay. I accept your protection. When does it start?"

"Fifteen minutes ago," Simon said. "I'm glad you agreed to let us help, because I was going to be with you whether you wanted me to or not."

She cocked an eyebrow. "Is that right? And I wouldn't have had a say in it?"

"You did have a say," he pointed out. "Since you

agreed, I won't have to sneak around and provide your protection covertly." He grinned. "Now, do you ride with me, or should I follow you to your place?"

Holly wasn't sure she liked that he'd already decided to provide her protection without her permission. But then, there was that message on the windshield... "You can follow me," she said, unwilling to give up every bit of her independence.

He nodded. "But first, let's clear up one thing."

She lifted her chin, stiffened and prepared to do verbal battle with the man who was going to spend who knew how long with her—at least until she figured out how to break the curse.

But he didn't say a word. Instead, he leaned into her car and switched on the windshield wipers. Two seconds later, the message was swept away.

The starch left her body as she faced the open door, the driver's seat and the car she'd always loved driving. Until now. The message was gone, but it lingered in her thoughts.

Simon touched her elbow. "Ride with me," he whispered. "Let's get a mechanic to look over your car to make sure the message wasn't the only thing left behind."

"Right," Remy said. "I'll have a tow truck take your car to a mechanic I know."

If she hadn't been so hesitant to get back into her car, she'd have blasted them for railroading her into riding with Simon.

"Okay." Holly hated how pathetic she sounded. To make up for it, she added in a more forceful tone, "But just until they give my car the once-over."

"You two going to be all right?" Remy asked. "I could follow you to Holly's place as well."

"We don't even know if the words mean more than just words," Holly shook her head. "One shadow is all I can handle for now."

Remy grinned. "Got it. All you have to do is call if you need reinforcements."

"Thank you," Holly said, suddenly tired to the bone. She turned to Simon. "I'm ready, if you are." To Remy, she added, "Keys are in the ignition."

"We'll take care of it." Remy leaned into the car, shut off the engine and came out with a frown denting his forehead. "Does this look familiar?" He held up a small doll, handcrafted from brown twine wrapped mummy-style. Stuck in the doll's heart was a single pin with a black plastic skull affixed to it.

Holly's breath hitched. "I've never seen that before. It wasn't in my car when I arrived for my shift." She reluctantly held out her hand.

Remy placed the doll in her hand. "I take it that's another message."

She nodded.

"Do you want me to see if my contacts at the state crime lab can run tests on it?"

She shook her head. "I'd like to take it to my Mémère." At the very least, the resident Voodoo queen would confirm what Holly suspected. The doll was a warning. How much of a warning, she didn't want to admit. Based on the location of the pin stick, it could well be a death threat. She palmed the doll, careful not to dislodge the pin. Holly couldn't wait any longer. If her grandmother wasn't home the next day, she'd have to find her.

"It's just a doll," Simon whispered close to her ear.

He didn't understand what that doll represented. It was all part of the curse she'd come back to vanquish.

She didn't bother trying to convince him to believe in the power of black magic. He would be of no help in her attempt to remove the curse. But he would prove useful if he could protect her long enough to reverse the dark magic.

With that warm hand still at the small of her back, Simon guided her to his pickup and held open the passenger door for her.

She stepped up onto the running board and slid into the seat, glad to be off her feet for the first time in eight hours. The doll in her palm mocked her attempt to relax.

Having Simon so close wasn't helping either. He was far too attractive.

As tired as she was, she should have had no problem keeping everything on a professional basis. Even exhaustion wasn't helping her focus on what mattered—*Removing the curse.*

Not dancing with Simon or imagining his big body filling the limited space in her houseboat.

What she needed was a cool shower, a soft bed and sleep.

She leaned her head back against the seat, closed her eyes and waited for Simon to close the door.

The truck dipped slightly, and something whispered across her breast.

Holly's eyes shot open to find Simon leaning over her.

"What the hell?" she muttered. Everywhere he brushed against her lit up like the fourth of July, sending electrical shocks throughout her body.

"Just buckling you in," he said as he stretched the shoulder strap over her and snapped the buckle in place, his knuckles grazing her hip.

Sweet Jesus.

In that brief moment, she went from near-death exhaustion to all her senses on high alert.

If her breath wasn't lodged in her lungs, Holly would have told him to never mind. She could drive her own car and take care of her own self. Twenty-four-seven with the man who could dance and who sent her senses into a raging whirlwind by simply buckling her seatbelt was a bad idea.

She reminded herself that it was a good thing she wasn't in the market for a relationship.

Now, she just had to keep repeating that thought

to herself or risk putting the man in jeopardy of her deadly curse.

And if her self-coaching didn't do it, the doll in her hand should be enough of a reminder of the trouble she was in and, by association, everyone around her could be affected.

CHAPTER 4

SIMON FOLLOWED Holly's directions through town and down a road that ran along the edge of the bayou. They turned onto a narrow gravel path lined by oak trees dripping with Spanish moss.

Creepy at night, Simon could imagine it wasn't much better in daylight. Eventually, they emerged into a small clearing. Simon slowed to a stop. Straight ahead, the headlights glinted off the inky waters of the bayou. Expecting a house, Simon was surprised to find only a houseboat moored to a dock, with a single light shining over the door onto the dock.

"You live on a houseboat?" he asked.

She smiled. "As of today. Do you know how hard it is to find a house to rent at this time of year?"

"Actually, I do," he said. "Which reminds me, I

have an appointment with a real estate agent tomorrow. I'll need to cancel."

Holly frowned across the console at him. "Why do you have to cancel?"

"I'm on assignment. I won't leave you alone while I'm out house hunting."

Her lips pressed together. "What time is your appointment?"

"Ten o'clock. I'm sure it won't be a problem to push it off for a few weeks."

"Good grief. I don't have to be at work until tomorrow afternoon at five. Keep your appointment. I'll go with you. Who knows? Maybe I'll see something I like."

Simon frowned as Holly shot down his excuse to cancel. He'd been in the small town since the Bayou Brotherhood Protectors had formed and had yet to look for a place to live. He hadn't been entirely certain he wanted to stay. "Are you sure?"

"Positive. I didn't relish spending the entire day cleaning or waiting to hear from my Mémère. I need to get out and see what's changed in this town since I've been gone."

Simon sighed. "Okay. We'll go house hunting tomorrow morning."

"After that, if she hasn't contacted me, I'd like to see if my Mémère is home and ready to help."

He nodded. "We can do that." Though he didn't believe in curses or Voodoo, he was interested in meeting Bayou Mambaloa's very own Voodoo queen. He'd found the Louisiana bayous full of interesting characters. Most friendly. Some not so much.

Simon shifted into park and cut the engine. Then he dropped to the ground, grabbed the go-bag he kept behind the back seat and hurried around to open Holly's door. She was already out and joined him in front of the truck.

For a moment, Holly stood staring at the houseboat. Finally, she shrugged. "It needs a good cleaning and minor maintenance. The engine doesn't actually work, but I don't need it to go anywhere. The best part was that it was in my budget and available." She shot a glance his way. "However, it only has one bed." She grimaced. "You'll have to camp out on the couch."

"I'll manage," he said.

"You haven't seen the couch," she muttered beneath her breath and led the way to the dock.

They came to a stop on the dock, where a gangway led to the houseboat. An anchor lay on the dock next to a metal storage box. Simon held out his hand. "Let me have the key. I want to do a quick check before you go inside."

She bent, tipped the anchor to the side, reached for something then straightened, handing him a key.

Simon closed his eyes for a second. "Please tell me this isn't the key to the houseboat."

"Okay," she said. "I won't tell you. But if you want

to open the door, you'll have to use whatever that is in your hand."

He shook his head. "Tomorrow, we're going to the hardware store for new locks."

She sighed. "I'll agree with you on that. Remember, I just moved in today."

"Wherever you were staying before, perhaps we should stay there tonight."

"That was at my Mémère's. She's been away for a few days helping others."

"Why aren't you staying there still?"

"Now that I have a job, I like to get there without taking a boat through the bayou at night after I get off work." She crossed the gangway and stood beside the door.

Simon followed, stuck the key in the lock and pushed the door open.

Holly reached around him and flipped a light switch, illuminating the interior with soft, warm light.

"Give me a minute inside," he said. "I just want to make sure it's safe."

"And standing out in the open is safer?" she asked with one eyebrow cocked.

He frowned. "Fine." He leaned into the door, peered around and didn't see anything moving. "Come in, but stand next to the door while I look around."

"That won't take long," she murmured. "It's not

that big, and there aren't many places for anyone to hide."

"Humor me," he said through clenched teeth.

She stepped into the house, closed the door behind her and leaned against the wall. "Go on. I'm humoring."

He wanted to be mad at her, but her sassy smirk only made him want to kiss her. That thought made him mad at himself. He had no business kissing the client. And that was all she was to him. All she could be. A client.

Especially after his relapse on the PTSD front. Whatever happened while he was with her, he had to focus on the present and not let anything transport him back to Syria. He couldn't change anything about the past. But if he kept his wits about him, he could have an impact on the future. He'd do his best to make it a positive impact. His job was to protect Holly Hazard.

He dropped his go-bag by the door and performed his safety check.

As she'd predicted, it didn't take him more than a minute to search the entire houseboat. No bad guys lay in wait to jump out in a surprise attack. There were no hiding places on board. Every inch of space was a testament to efficient storage.

The bottom floor had a cozy living space opening to a kitchenette with just enough of a stove and oven to make a meal. An open door on the other side of the kitchenette led to a bathroom with a toilet and a tub-shower unit. Thankfully, it was close to full size. Two people could manage an intimate shower in it.

Don't go there, man. Hands and mind off the client.

"Downstairs is clear," he said.

The only bedroom was more of a loft at the top of a narrow staircase. At least the ceiling was high enough that Simon could stand straight without bumping his head. A stack of sheets waited to be spread across the mattress. One more thing for Holly to do before she could call it a night.

A single closet was too small for a person to hide in, and the space beneath the bed had been fashioned into drawers. Windows all around looked out on the bayou, where starlight reflected like a blanket of diamonds on the dark water.

Simon hurried back down to find Holly pulling clothing out of a suitcase.

"I'd like to shower first, if you don't mind," she said. "I still feel sticky from the spilled beer."

"Go for it. I can wait."

After she disappeared into the bathroom, he climbed the stairs and made the bed, smoothing sheets over the mattress and topping it with a light comforter. The houseboat was equipped with an air conditioner. He adjusted the thermostat to a cooler setting to combat the humidity.

He fluffed the pillow in its freshly laundered pillowcase and leaned it against the headboard.

SIMON

Housekeeping wasn't part of the job, but his father had taught him that making a woman's life easier was part of showing her respect. His father had always helped his mother with household chores, as well as maintaining the yard and vehicles.

He grabbed one of the two pillows and a spare sheet he found in a drawer beneath the bed and carried them down the stairs.

Holly emerged from the bathroom, wearing short shorts and a loose T-shirt. She'd combed her auburn hair straight back from her forehead. Long, damp strands hung down to the middle of her back. With her face shiny clean and free of makeup, she looked young and fresh, her green eyes bright, despite the shadows beneath.

"Feel better?" he asked.

She smiled. "Much. It's all yours."

"I'll leave the door ajar. If you hear any noises outside the houseboat, let me know." He frowned. "Maybe I should wait and ask one of the guys to spell me so you're not compromised while I'm in the shower."

Holly laughed. "Don't be ridiculous. I'll stand guard on my bodyguard, if it makes you feel better."

He shook his head with a smile. "Or you could join me in the shower. That way, I'll be with you should you be attacked."

Her face flushed a pretty pink. "Nice try," she said,

her voice breathy, like she couldn't quite get enough air in her lungs.

"Either way, I'm leaving the bathroom door open," he said. "Don't open the door to the houseboat for anyone. I'll only be a minute."

She waved him away. "Go on. I'll be fine."

For a moment, he hesitated. "Okay then."

Simon ducked into the bathroom, fired up the shower and hurried to finish.

Still dripping wet, he stepped out of the shower less than three minutes later, flinging water from his hair.

She sat on the couch, a smile pulling at the corners of her lips. "Still here. No bad guys," she said.

Simon released the breath he'd held throughout the brief shower. "Good." He tipped his chin toward the staircase. "Goodnight then."

Holly placed her foot on the bottom step. "Goodnight, Simon Sevier." Her brief smile warmed him. "Thank you for coming to my rescue tonight."

"It was my pleasure."

"You're a good guy," she said.

"I don't know about that."

"Trust me," she said. "You are. I just hope that helping me doesn't make you the next target of my curse."

"As I don't believe in magic, Voodoo, luck or curses, I think I'll be all right. Don't worry about me. I'm here to take care of you."

She stared at him for a long moment before she nodded. "Curses can be complicated. I'll do my best to take care of you as well."

"Thank you." He didn't bother to refute her offer to look out for him. If it made her feel better to think she could help with her belief in Voodoo and magic, it wasn't up to him to burst her bubble or pooh-pooh her ideology. Instead, he held up his hand for a high-five. "I'll have your back, and you'll have mine. Teamwork."

"Teamwork," she echoed as she clapped her palm to his. Her brow furrowed. "You'll be okay on the couch?" Her gaze focused on the small sofa in the cozy but tight living area. "There's no way you'll be able to stretch out on that."

"I'll be fine," he insisted. He'd probably have to drape his legs over the armrests, but it was still better than sleeping in a foxhole or nodding off in the back of an armored personnel carrier. "Go to sleep. We have a busy day tomorrow."

She nodded. "House hunting."

"Then a visit to the Voodoo queen."

"And I have to work tomorrow evening," Holly added.

"I can cancel the house hunting," he reminded her.

"No. That's the one thing I'm looking forward to." She went up another step. "Good night, Simon. Thanks for a memorable evening."

He gave her a mock salute. "My pleasure."

Holly disappeared into the loft bedroom.

Simon checked all the windows and the door one more time before he settled on the sofa.

It had been an interesting day, from welding seams on a jon boat to reliving the worst day of his life in Syria, to coming to the rescue of a beautiful woman who believed in magic.

Simon punched the pillow several times, then lay back, his legs hanging over the arms of the sofa. He reminded himself he'd slept in worse places in the many years he'd been a Delta Force soldier. But damn, he wasn't getting any younger.

Sounds of Holly moving about in the loft bedroom drifted to him.

He didn't care that he couldn't get comfortable. The woman in the bed at the top of the stairs had been threatened. Her life could very well be in danger.

Simon was on the hook for seeing to her safety. He couldn't drop the ball. Couldn't let anyone get past him to her. He was her last line of defense. He'd failed Johnny back in Syria. He couldn't fail Holly in Bayou Mambaloa.

Though he closed his eyes and lay his head on the soft pillow, he opened his senses and remained on alert, listening and feeling the motion of the boat. He vowed to himself, and silently to Holly, that he would be ready to defend.

The rustling of bed sheets had him imagining Holly settling into the bed.

"Simon?" her voice called out.

"Yeah."

"Thank you for making the bed," she said softly.

He smiled in the darkness. "You're welcome."

Silence stretched between them.

"Simon?"

"Yeah."

"This is a big bed. It's big enough we could share it," she said. "No need to suffer on the couch."

Oh, he was tempted. "I'm fine, Holly."

"Seriously. It doesn't have to mean anything other than a good night's sleep."

"I'm fine," he said, though his voice was tight as he fought to maintain control of his desire to climb the ridiculously narrow stairs to the loft over his head. "Go to sleep, Holly."

"Simon?"

He counted to five before responding. "Yeah."

"Your mama taught you well."

If Holly only knew how much he wanted to take her up on the offer to share her bed...

It was just as well, she didn't.

She was the client.

He was a damaged ex-soldier with PTSD issues.

It would be best to keep his distance from the pretty bayou babe who believed in Voodoo and magic.

CHAPTER 5

Tired from being on her feet for eight hours, Holly expected to sleep as soon as her head hit the pillow.

That didn't happen.

She lay still, staring at the starlight reflected off the bayou, dancing across the ceiling. Every noise drew her attention. Not because of the possible danger she could be in, but because of the really hot guy lying across her couch below. Her curiosity burned in her veins, making her wonder what he wore to sleep. If he even wore anything.

Her core flamed, and her curiosity got the better of her. Easing out of the bed proved to be noisier than she'd anticipated. She'd barely rolled over when the bedframe creaked.

After pausing for a moment of silence and a chance to listen, Holly moved again, sliding off the bed onto the floor where she crawled to the edge of the loft, rose on her knees and peered over the rail.

Simon lay on his back, his hands laced behind his head, wearing only a pair of shorts, his bare, muscular chest a shadowy blue in the limited light filtering through the windows. "Everything all right up there?" His voice cut through the shadows, startling Holly.

"Yes. Yes, of course," she said. "However, you don't look very comfortable."

"I'm great," he said.

"If you were so great, why are you still awake?"

"I could ask you the same," he shot back at her, though his tone was soft.

"I can't stop thinking about everything that happened tonight," she said, lingering at the rail, not ready to go back to bed when she could stare down at masculine perfection.

Perfection she couldn't touch. But it didn't hurt to look.

"Cody won't bother you again. You've proven you can take care of yourself."

"Cody wasn't always such a bully. I don't know why he all of a sudden thinks I should belong to him. He never pushed the limits when Paul and I were dating. Then again, I didn't stick around after Paul died."

"I'm sorry about your boyfriend," Simon said.

"And your parents. That had to be hard to lose them all so close together.

She nodded, though he probably couldn't see the movement in the murky darkness. "It was hard. But with Paul, I went to his funeral. Saw him at the viewing. He was well and truly dead. My parents' boat capsized. Their bodies were never recovered."

"Dead is dead. Permanent," he said. "But no bodies? No proof of death? It leaves a glimmer of hope that they're still alive."

"Yeah," she whispered. "If they are...why haven't they tried to contact me?"

"Maybe they can't."

"Do you think they could be held captive somewhere? That for the last six months they've been unable to get word out that they're alive?" Holly had prayed every day since their boat had been found that one day they'd show up after having been rescued from a deserted island.

As time had passed, hope had turned to despair. If they'd died, she'd have mourned their loss and eventually gotten on with her life.

"You're probably in a constant flux of grief or hope. It's hard to focus on regular, day-to-day existence."

"Yeah." It had been hard to just move on. "Part of it is that I feel like I should've done more to stop those things from happening. I should've convinced Paul not to go to New Orleans that morning. I should've gone to folks as soon as I saw the message in the sand."

"No amount of regret or second-guessing can change the past. Yet we wallow in it, sabotaging our chances at a future, at happiness."

His words echoed exactly what she'd felt over the last six months. "Yet, we hold onto the guilt, afraid to let go."

"That by letting go, you aren't repenting for your failure to keep them alive, or you aren't showing them the love and respect they deserve by keeping them foremost in your heart and mind."

"Wow. That's deep," she said. "You speak as if from experience. From your own loss."

His silence was answer enough.

"I'm sorry for your loss," she said softly, "whoever he or she was."

"He. Johnny," Simon said. "We were battle buddies. We were supposed to have each other's backs."

"What happened?"

"I should've had his front that day. I should've taken point," Simon's voice faded. Silence stretched for a moment. "He had a wife and son. I didn't have anyone depending on me to come home. I shouldn't have let him take the lead. Had I gone first, Johnny would be home with his wife and son."

"And he would've been wondering if he'd done enough to keep you from dying." Holly sighed.

"Hindsight is too late. Again, you can't change the past."

"Reliving it over and over won't make it better," Simon said. "It makes for a miserable present and future."

"There's nothing like late-night discussions on philosophy." Holly yawned, surprised that her discussion over the rail with Simon, no matter how deep and sad, had eased the tension she hadn't been able to shake since she'd seen the message on the mirror in her Atlanta apartment.

"We can't change the world tonight," Simon's smooth, deep tone floated up to her perch in the loft. "We'll work on it tomorrow."

She crawled up on the bed, pulled the comforter up to her chin and closed her eyes, relieved she wasn't alone. And though she'd always clung fiercely to her independence, she was glad it was Simon providing her protection.

It seemed no sooner had she closed her eyes than she woke to sunlight streaming through the windows. The rich aroma of fresh-brewed coffee filled her senses, urging her to get up and go in search of a cup and the man who was brewing it.

Holly finger-combed her hair, hoping she didn't look as bedraggled as usual. If this arrangement lasted more than a day or two, she'd have to bring a brush to the loft and find more suitable sleeping arrangements for her bodyguard.

She dug into the small closet for a pair of jeans and a ribbed knit pullover, the color of an eggplant. The shirt hugged her like a second skin, accentuating the swell of her breasts and her narrow waist.

As she descended the stairs, her bare feet made no sound, giving her the opportunity to study the man pouring coffee into a mug.

He'd changed from the shorts into a pair of jeans but had yet to hide his broad shoulders under a shirt. Daylight gave his skin a golden glow. Every movement was a study in flexing muscles.

Having danced with him the previous night, Holly was fully aware of how solid he was. Still, her fingers itched to feel the warmth of his skin stretched over those taut muscles.

Her mouth watered, heat rushed up her chest into her cheeks and her core flamed with unexpected desire.

Simon chose that moment to turn. Though he wore the jeans fully zipped, the top button hadn't been secured. To Holly, it represented full-on temptation. Add the sexy smile spreading across his face, and the man was chipping away at her resistance. "Perfect timing," he said. "You can have the first cup while I find a shirt."

"Oh, no hurry," she was too quick to say. "I mean,

about the coffee. You made it, you deserve the first cup."

His lips twisted. "Damn, and I was hoping you'd be the guinea pig and test it before I poured one for me." He winked.

"No, really. I want to duck into the bathroom. I need to tame my bed hair before I frighten the natives."

His gaze swept over her face and hair. "You look beautiful and refreshed."

"Liar on the beautiful," she said. "Is refreshed code for interesting. You know, that word you use when you aren't impressed, but don't want to be rude?"

Simon laughed. "You *are* beautiful, and you look well rested. The dark circles under your eyes have faded."

Holly touched her fingers to her face. "They were pretty bad, weren't they?" She grimaced. "It's all a result of no sleep and waiting for the next shoe to drop on the curse that's been plaguing me for the last six months. But thanks to you, I slept well last night —sadly, at your expense."

"I managed to sleep," he said. "Despite being about two feet too short, the sofa was soft enough for me to get semi-comfortable."

With a frown, Holly studied the offending piece of furniture. "We need to do something about that. A man your size can't sleep like that every night. I can't even stretch out on the couch, and I'm at least six inches shorter than you."

Simon shook his head. "I can manage. Go. Do your morning thing. I'll see what I can whip up for breakfast."

Her eyebrows rose. "You protect and cook? I should've hired a Brotherhood Protector ages ago."

He tossed a hand towel at her. "Keep it up, and you can make your own breakfast."

Holly squeezed by him, her hip brushing against his on her way through the kitchen to the bathroom.

Once she was inside with the door closed, she stared into the mirror at a woman with pink cheeks and a sparkle in her eye. She'd enjoyed sparring with her bodyguard. And the view had been better than average.

Hell, who was she kidding? The man was drool-worthy. It had been all she could do not to run her fingers over his shoulders as she'd moved past him.

After brushing her teeth, she smoothed the tangles from her thick hair and pulled it up into a loose bun on top of her head. As an afterthought, she loosened a few stray tendrils to curl around her ears.

A little mascara and a dab of lipstick were all she needed, and she stepped out of the bathroom to find Simon fully dressed in a clean T-shirt and boots, scooping fluffy yellow scrambled eggs out of a skillet onto two plates. When toast popped up out of the toaster, he added a piece to each plate, along with a fork, and handed one to her.

Simon nodded to the sliding glass doors that led off the living room onto a patio area overlooking the bayou. "Shall we eat on the deck?"

"Absolutely," Holly said. "It was one of the selling points for renting here instead of a house in town. That and availability."

Simon led the way, flicked the lock open and slid the door open. Then he moved to the side, allowing her to pass through first.

The morning sun still hung low on the horizon, blocked by towering cypress trees. In another hour, the sun would crest the treetops and shine directly down, raising the temperature and the humidity. But at that moment, being outside was tolerable, the view was beautiful and the bayou peaceful. Soon, charter fishing boats and airboats with their massive fans would be passing by, carrying tourists out into the bayou.

Holly sank onto one of the cushioned chairs and laid her plate on the tiny bistro table.

Simon set his plate on the other side. "Don't go anywhere. I'll be right back."

Her gaze followed him as he disappeared through the door and reappeared a moment later, carrying two steaming mugs of coffee.

She took one from him and sniffed appreciatively.

"This is my drug of choice," she murmured as she took a careful sip.

They spent the next few minutes devouring the scrambled eggs and toast. When her plate was empty, Holly sighed and sat back with her coffee. "That was good. Thank you."

He dipped his head.

"You don't have to cook for me, you know."

"I know. But I like to start my day with a good breakfast. It was no big deal to make enough for two."

"I'll make it tomorrow," she said. "As long as eggs are good for you two days in a row."

"Every day is a good day for eggs." He brought his mug to his lips and drank.

"So, house hunting, huh?" Holly tipped her head and stared at Simon. "Do you have an idea of what you'd like to find?"

"None," he said.

Holly's lips twitched on the corners. "You'll know it when you see it?"

"I hope." He shrugged.

She studied him over the top of her coffee cup. "You don't sound very enthusiastic about it."

"I'm not."

"Then why are you looking?"

His lips pressed together. "I've been living in the old boarding house since my team was established here. It's a great temporary place to live. Remy wanted a place where new recruits to our team could stay until they could find more permanent lodging."

"And you've overstayed the temporary part." Her brow dipped. "Is Remy kicking you out?"

Simon chuckled. "Not at all."

"So, why now?"

"After years in the Army, I never bothered buying a home. If I had, I would've had to sell it when I moved to my next duty station. It was easier renting—and easier still to rent furnished apartments. That way, all I had to pack was clothes and a few personal items, all of which fit in my truck. I could punch out and be on the road in under two hours."

"No roots?"

He shook his head.

"What about settling close to your folks?"

Simon chuckled. "After they left the military, they moved back to their hometown in Michigan."

"Why didn't you find a place close to them?"

"They didn't last long in Michigan. After twenty-plus years of moving around in the military, staying in one place almost drove them nuts. They've taken the concept of no roots to the next level."

"How so?"

"They sold their house, bought a motorhome and travel the continent. They're somewhere in British Columbia now, making their way slowly to Alaska on the ALCAN Highway."

"Do you aspire to the motorhome, nomad's life?"

Holly asked. "Is that why you're hesitant to purchase a house?"

"Good lord, no." He shrugged and stared out at the bayou. "I guess in all the places I've been, no one place made me feel like it was home."

Holly nodded. "I didn't get that concept until I left the only home I'd ever known and moved to Atlanta. I might not have moved as many times as you, but I learned a lot about myself in that one move."

His gaze met hers. "And what did you learn?"

"It's not the place that makes it home." Holly smiled. "It's the people you connect with. Your friends and family." Her brow wrinkled. "I lost my parents to a boating accident. I lost my home by leaving my friends and extended family and moving to Atlanta."

"And now that you're back?"

Her lips spread in a wistful smile. "This is home." Holly's jaw hardened. "I just hope I haven't endangered my friends and family by coming back. I'm tired of being alone in a city that doesn't know me or give a rat's ass whether I live or die. I'm home and mean to stay. Which makes it all the more imperative that I find and neutralize whatever or whoever is threatening me."

"I'm here to help. We can tap into my team's resources as well. We have a couple of computer gurus who are experts at mining data to find even the most obscure sources of information to help us solve cases—Swede in Eagle Rock, Montana, and Kyla in West Yellowstone. I'd like to get Swede searching for information about your parents. I can forward their names to him and get him started."

"Don't judge me if I don't get all excited. I hopped on that rollercoaster every time the sheriff's department came up with any new data concerning their whereabouts. Each time, it led nowhere. I can't imagine your Swede finding anything different from what the sheriff chased. All his leads went nowhere. My parents are still missing and presumed dead."

"It hurts to hit walls in your search for the truth, but give Swede the benefit of the doubt. He's a master."

Holly cocked a brow. "Hacker?"

Simon shrugged. "Master...hacker...whatever gets the job done. The main takeaway is that Swede is one of the good guys. He only goes after data that will save lives."

"That's reassuring," Holly said, though not entirely reassured.

Simon glanced at his watch. "I'm supposed to meet the realtor in fifteen minutes. Can you be ready in ten?"

"I just need to brush my teeth and put on my shoes." She rose and started to collect their plates.

Simon took them from her. "I'll clean up while you find your shoes."

"But you cooked. That means I clean."

"Normally, I'd agree, but I'll do it this time."

"He's a bodyguard, a cook and chief bottle-washer. A woman could fall in love with a man like that," she muttered as she stepped back into the houseboat. A little louder, she said, "Doesn't get better than that.

Falling in love with Simon was completely out of the question, off the table, wiped clean from her mind.

Uh-huh. Now that the thought was there, it wouldn't go away.

Stop now. She was not going to fall in love with Simon. And as for having a man in her life that did all the things he did and was probably good in bed, well...

Don't get used to it.

CHAPTER 6

Don't get used to it.

Holly repeated this mantra in her mind, which was better than repeating, "Don't fall in love," over and over. She was afraid that if she did, the idea would become ingrained and she'd obsess over trying to free her thoughts of love, a house with a picket fence and half a dozen children playing in the yard. It didn't help that she'd agreed to go house hunting with the man.

Fifteen minutes later, they pulled up at the address the realtor had texted to Simon.

A sleek, black SUV was parked in the driveway. As Simon brought his truck to a halt, a tall, dark woman emerged from the house dressed in a cream-colored pantsuit that complemented her sultry dark skin. Standing on the top step in three-inch, shiny gold stilettoes, with a chunky necklace and belt that matched her shoes, she looked like a model from a fashion magazine. If it were anyone else but LaShawnda Jones, Holly might have been intimidated.

"LaLa," she called out and hurried up the stairs to hug the woman. "Simon didn't tell me you were his realtor."

"Mr. Sevier didn't tell me he was bringing my sweet Holly Lolly." LaShawnda returned the hug, then straightened and held out her hand. "And you must be Mr. Sinclaire Simon Sevier. So nice to meet you in person."

"Oh, you two haven't met?" Holly asked.

"We spoke on the phone," Simon said and shook LaShawnda's beautifully manicured hand. "It's a pleasure to meet you, ma'am."

"Oh, please, darlin', don't call me ma'am. Makes me feel decades older. And I'm not ready for that travesty." She released his hand and stared from him to Holly. "You said you were looking for a modest home. Not too big, not too little. That leaves your options open for just about anything. I've lined up a few properties, but it would really help if you could narrow it down a bit."

"I've never bought a house," Simon said. "I've only ever lived in apartments and now the boarding house. I'm not even sure what to consider."

"It's always good to get the opinion of the woman with whom you will be sharing your abode." She tipped her head toward Holly. "You're one step ahead of some by including your woman in the decision-making process."

Holly shook her head. "Oh, we're not buying a house together."

"No?" LaShawnda raised a beautifully arched brow. "What a shame, Holly Lolly. He's such a delicious specimen. Still, a woman's opinion is always good to have in choosing a home. If you follow me, I'll show you the first on our agenda."

She led them through the midcentury modern home, which had been remodeled with new wood flooring and an updated kitchen with gold accents and hardware. It was stark, a little masculine and cold.

By the time they stepped back out on the porch, Holly had made up her mind. But this would be Simon's home, not hers, so she waited to get his take.

"So, Mr. Sevier," LaShawnda waved a hand toward the home. "What did you think?"

"It's a house. I liked its clean lines and updated flooring. The yard's a little smaller than I would like."

"It is small if you want a dog or a few children."

Simon turned to Holly. "What did you think?"

She really didn't want her opinion to sway his decision, but he had asked. "I liked how they combined the old style with more modern sleekness, but it reminded me more of a posh doctor's office than a home. I would feel like I couldn't relax in a place like that. But that's just me. You might feel perfectly comfortable here."

Simon stared at the house, his eyes narrowing. Then he turned to LaShawnda. "What else do you have?"

She smiled and waved a hand toward the stairs. "If you'll follow me, I'll show you."

They visited three more homes, each having pros and cons. None felt like home to Holly.

"I'll find more for our next visit," LaShawnda said. "Will you be available tomorrow for a couple of hours in the morning?"

Simon frowned and met Holly's gaze.

"I don't work tomorrow. If you want to look for a house, I can go along with you again. Although I don't know that I've been much help."

LaShawnda tilted her head and cocked an eyebrow. "Did you find a house today that made you feel at home?"

Holly shook her head and transferred her gaze to Simon. "Did you?"

His lip pressed together. "I'm not sure what that feels like anymore."

"It's simple," LaShawnda said. "Did any of the houses make you want to go in, kick off your shoes and let go of the breath you've been holding all day?"

Simon laughed. "No."

The realtor clapped her hands together. "Then we'll keep looking. I'll line up a few more for tomorrow. In the meantime, you two should come up with a list of what you think of when you think of a home. Go through each room in your mind. What makes you think of home in a living room? What in a kitchen gives you warm fuzzies? Do you need a soaker tub to make your bathroom complete?" She smiled. "You get the idea."

Holly could envision all those things, but she didn't want to remind LaShawnda that her opinion didn't matter. This would be Simon's house. Not hers.

"So, tomorrow? Same time?" the realtor asked.

Simon met Holly's gaze.

Holly nodded. "Sounds good."

"I'll text our starting address." LaShawnda hugged Holly. "I'm glad you're home." Then she held out a hand to Simon. "You two will find the perfect house. I'm sure of it."

Then she was gone, leaving Holly and Simon standing in front of the last house they'd toured.

Simon sighed. "House hunting is more painful than low-crawling through a mud pit."

Holly grinned. "At least it's not as dirty. Let's go see Madam Gautier. Maybe we'll be more successful countering my curse."

After they climbed into the truck, Simon turned to Holly. "Your grandmother lives on an island in the bayou?"

"She does," Holly said. "We can borrow a skiff

from Mitch at the marina. My grandmother has her own, but it'll be with her, whether she's home or out visiting sick neighbors."

Simon drove to the marina and parked the truck in the parking lot.

Being summer, the lot was full of people coming and going.

Inside the marina store, Holly found Mitchell Marceau behind the bait counter, fishing minnows out of a tank to fill a plastic bag for a customer. The scene was exactly what Holly would have expected, except for who was holding the plastic bag.

Principal Joyce Ashcraft glanced up and grinned. "Well, good morning, Holly," she said. "Mitch is showing me how to package bait. He's promised to teach me how to fish later this evening when he closes up shop."

"You've never been fishing?" Holly asked.

"I know. Sounds incredible." Joyce's grin twisted. "I've lived so many years on the bayou and have never gone fishing."

Mitch shook his head. "She hasn't even dropped a line from a cane pole while standing on the bank."

Joyce shrugged. "My dad died when I was young, and Mom wasn't much for the outdoors. But Mitch has agreed to show me the ropes. We might even go frog-gigging." She grimaced. "Though I might let him handle the frogs."

Mitchell wrapped a twist tie around the mouth of

the plastic bag and handed it to the man waiting patiently. He wiped his hands on the apron he wore, came around from behind the tank and met Holly's gaze. "What can I help you with?"

"I need a skiff to get out to Mémère's house. Do you have one available?"

"All my rentals are out, but you can take mine," Mitchell said. "You remember where I keep it?"

Holly smiled. "I do. Thanks, Mitch."

His brow furrowed. "I heard you had another message on your vehicle last night."

Her smile slipping, Holly nodded. "Yes, sir. Writing on the window and a voodoo doll on my passenger seat."

Mitch's frown deepened. "Voodoo isn't something to play around with."

"You believe Voodoo is real?" Joyce asked Mitchell.

He nodded, solemnly. "I didn't until Holly's grandmother helped me break a curse one of the Fontenots put on my marina a decade ago. Almost lost everything until she did her thing and turned my life and business around. I owe that woman." He tipped his head toward Holly. "You be careful, now, ya hear? You, Gisele and Madam Gautier are good people. So were your parents. God rest their souls."

Holly's heart swelled, and tears burned her eyes. "Thank you, Mitch." She hugged the older man. "I'll be careful with your skiff and bring it back before this evening's fishing lesson."

He waved a hand. "No worries. I can always take one of the bass boats if you're not back soon enough."

"I have to be back for work anyway. I'm glad you're going to teach Ms. Ashcraft how to fish. I always loved fishing with my dad. Something about floating along the bayou with a fishing pole in your hand... It doesn't get better than that." Especially when it was with someone you loved. Her heart hitched at the memories of her and her father fishing at dusk, listening to frogs and cicadas making music in the bayou.

"Simon," Mitchell held out a hand, "I'm glad to hear you're looking after our girl. She's special, like her grandmother."

Simon shook the man's hand. "I'll keep an eye on her."

Holly led the way out onto the dock to the far end, where a small skiff was tied to a piling.

Simon looked at it suspiciously. "Is it big enough for both of us?"

She laughed. "Yes, of course. I'll get in first, if it makes you feel better."

"It does." He waited for her to step into the small craft and settle on the back bench. Once she was in, he eased into the boat and took a seat, without rocking it too badly.

"See? It's fine," she said and pulled the line to start

the engine. The outboard motor roared to life. With her hand on the tiller handle, she steered the boat away from the dock and out into the bayou.

"How long has your grandmother lived on her island in the bayou?" Simon asked.

"Most of her life," Holly answered. "She was born and raised there. She had a place on the mainland after she married and had children. Raised them all and moved back to the island when her mother passed. She took her place as the resident Voodoo queen."

"What exactly does the job of resident Voodoo queen entail?"

Holly smiled. "Mostly, she uses her skills with herbs and potions to help others with their problems."

"Problems like?"

"Usually health issues."

"Why don't they go to a doctor?"

Holly shook her head. "Many of them either have gone and gotten no relief or can't afford to go. Mémère helps them, whether or not they can afford to pay. She helps with emotional support as well. Sometimes, all they need is a shoulder to lean on. Someone who will bear witness to their love, loss or loneliness."

Holly wove in and out of the channels until she came to a small island. A short dock jutted out into the water with a skiff tied to a cleat on one of the pilings.

Relief filled Holly's heart. "Oh, good, she's home." She killed the engine and floated up to the dock.

When they were close, Simon reached out a hand and caught the edge, pulling the skiff alongside. Using the line at the front of the craft, he tied it to a piling and stepped up onto the weathered boardwalk.

He reached down, grasped Holly's hand and pulled her up beside him, slipping an arm around her waist to steady her.

She liked how strong and solid he was. For the moment, she wasn't in a hurry to move away.

"Holly, my dear girl," a voice called out from the porch of the house perched on a gentle rise above the dock.

Holly glanced up at Simon. "Fair warning...my Mémère can be direct, and sometimes, intimidating. Don't take her words personally. She really does wish most people well."

"Are there some she doesn't?"

Holly's lips twitched. "There have been a few who've gotten crossways with her. She has her own special way of handling them."

"With a curse?"

"Maybe."

"You go on," Simon said. "I'll tie off the boat and join you."

"Afraid of her?" Holly asked.

He grinned and echoed her own word, "Maybe."

With a smile on her face, Holly strode up the rise, taking in all that was familiar, from the colorful chickens pecking at the dirt to the vibrant paint scheme on the cottage she'd spent much of her childhood. The house itself was painted a glorious cerulean blue, representing peace, serenity and the spiritual realm. Windows and doors were trimmed in a bright saffron, indicating understanding, mental clarity, and open communication. The door and shutters were a bold chili-pepper red for strength, power and passion. Standing on the porch, wearing a flowing caftan of all those colors and more, with a matching scarf tied over her shock of white hair, was her grandmother.

Holly hurried up the steps and wrapped her arms around the woman she loved with all her heart. "Mémère, I've missed you so much."

The older woman held her tightly and patted her back. "About time you came home. You never should've left." She sniffed and pulled back. "What's this I hear that you changed your name to Hazard? What's that all about?"

Holly smiled down at her diminutive grandmother. "I'd hoped that by changing my name and moving to another state, the curse wouldn't find me."

"That's the biggest bunch of gator droppings I've ever heard. You're a Gautier, by birth and blood.

Hazard." She snorted. "You're not a Hazard. The curse isn't about you."

"But it is." Holly gripped her grandmother's hands. "I thought by moving that I could keep other people I love safe. And it worked for six months. Or at least, I thought it worked. Until another message appeared in my bathroom mirror in Atlanta. It was then that I realized it would follow me anywhere. I needed to come home and warn you, my friends and family, that it was back."

"Hogwash, my dear. You should've stayed. I would've insisted that you come back, but you were grieving. I thought being away from what happened might help you move past your loss." She curled her fingers around her granddaughter's and squeezed. "But, Holly, my dear, sweet girl, you can't run away from your problems. You have to stay and fight."

Holly nodded, tears welling. "I know that now. I hope you can help me."

"You can tell me all about it after you introduce me to the fine, sturdy oak of a man headed this way." She leaned around her granddaughter and called out, "Mind yourself. Napoleon doesn't like men."

Simon's brow dipped. "Napoleon?"

As if on cue, a flash of color flew across the yard, straight at Simon, and attacked his legs.

"What the—" Simon danced around, trying to avoid a large, brown, blue, red and black rooster with a massive red comb.

"That's Napoleon," her grandmother said. "You know what to do."

Holly chuckled and reached for the large fish net hanging on a hook on a post and hurried out into the yard.

"Can you call it off?" he cried out.

"He's only protecting his hens," Holly said.

"Watch out," Simon moved to stand between her and the rooster. "His talons hurt."

Holly touched Simon's arm. "Move aside. I've got him."

"But he won't stop,"

"He will," she assured him.

Simon refused to let her by, all the while the rooster continued his attack. Simon continued to dance and kick as the rooster flapped his way backward and then quickly darted forward to sink his spurs into the man.

Holly stepped around Simon, scooped the rooster up in the fish net and carried it to the porch, where she hung the net, rooster and all, on the hook. "He won't bother you now. Come. Meet my Mémère." She ascended the steps and stood beside her grandmother, whose lips were twitching as if she fought a smile.

Simon brushed dust from his jeans and mounted the steps, steering clear of the rooster trapped in the fishnet.

Holly waved a hand toward her grandmother.

"Simon, this is my Mémère, Madam Gautier. Gran, this is Simon Sevier, my...bodyguard."

Her grandmother's eyes widened as she held out her hand. "Bodyguard, is it?"

Simon smiled as he took her hand and gently shook it. "Yes, ma'am. Until we find out who left the messages and the voodoo doll and put an end to the threats, I'll be with your granddaughter."

"Twenty-four-seven?" Madam Gautier's eyes narrowed.

"Yes, ma'am."

For a moment, she met and held Simon's gaze, using her famous stink-eye intimidating stare.

Holly almost laughed, but didn't because she was impressed with how Simon held his own, refusing to blink or look away.

Finally, Madam Gautier nodded. "All right then. I'm glad someone will help to protect my granddaughter. Now, tell me everything."

Holly told her about the message on the car the night before and gently pulled the voodoo doll out of her pocket, the pin still stuck firmly in the doll's body.

Madam Gautier took the doll in her hand and studied it for a long moment. Then she handed it back to Holly. "Cheap trick."

"What do you mean?" Holly asked.

Her grandmother turned the doll over, parted some of the twine and pointed.

Written in small letters, barely noticeable, were the words MADE IN CHINA.

Simon chuckled.

Holly shot a frown his way. "Okay, so it might not be part of the curse, but it is a threat."

"The only way that doll will hurt you is if you prick yourself with the pin, which is probably also made in China."

"What should I do?" Holly asked.

"Toss the doll in the garbage and go to work?" her grandmother said. "Has anyone shown any sign they aren't glad you're back in town?"

Holly shook her head. "The only person who has given me any grief is Cody West. He can't seem to accept that I have no desire to be with him. None. Zip. Nada."

"Caused you some trouble, did he?"

Holly nodded.

"Do you want me to put a curse on him?" Her Mémère's eyes shone with a sassy gleam. "Maybe give him a wicked itch that'll keep him busy for a while?"

Simon's lips twitched and then pressed together in a flat line. He leaned close to Holly and whispered, "Remind me not to make your grandmother mad."

Holly laughed. "That won't be necessary."

Her grandmother gave a solemn nod. "Find the person who isn't glad you're back, and you might find who put the doll in your car."

A shout sounded from the direction of the dock.

Simon, Holly and Madam Gautier turned to find someone paddling up in a pirogue.

Holly's eyes narrowed. "Is that Lissette?"

"Yoohoo," a feminine voice called out. The pirogue slid up the bank and came to a stop. As smooth as a dancer, Lissette stepped out, wearing a flowing dress, her long black hair falling down over her shoulders. Beautiful and unruffled after paddling through the bayou, she could just as easily have stepped off the runway at a fashion show.

"Who wears dresses to canoe through the bayou?" Holly muttered.

"Hi, y'all," Lissette sang as she sauntered up the rise carrying a basket like Little Red Riding Hood come to pay her grandmother a visit.

Only Lissette was more like the wolf than the little girl, always stirring up trouble and dragging everyone else into it.

The last thing she needed was Lissette to insert herself into her search for a cure to her curse.

Holly braced herself for whatever mischief Lissette came to serve up.

CHAPTER 7

Simon could sense the tension in Holly as her beautiful cousin strode across the grass like a vamp, without missing a step, a smile spreading across her face.

Instinctively, he didn't trust the woman. Simon moved closer to Holly and rested a hand lightly at the small of her back.

Holly shifted, without taking her eyes off her cousin, and leaned into his hand. He liked that she didn't pull away. Perhaps she was getting used to the idea of their ruse of being an item.

He was liking it more than he'd expected. House hunting with her had made the process a lot less painful. He'd appreciated her comments and views on the different homes they'd toured and found he'd agreed with everything she'd noted.

They had similar tastes in what they didn't like.

He hoped they were equally matched in what they did like.

Why that was important to him at that time, he didn't question. He just let it be.

"Ah, my Lissette," Madam Gautier said with a smile. "What brings you out in the bayou on such a lovely day?"

"You, of course." Lissette climbed the stairs, dropped a kiss on her grandmother's cheek and held out the basket. "I brought treats from the Bayou Bakery. I swear, Amelie makes the best eclairs in all of Louisiana. They are like her motto...baked with love." She folded back a cloth to display half a dozen of the sweet treats. "All for my sweet, little grandmama."

"You know eclairs are my favorite after Café Dumond's beignets." The Voodoo queen patted Lissette's cheek. "Thank you, my dear. Could you please put them on the counter in the kitchen? Then come join us on the porch."

"Yes, ma'am," Lissette said with a smile and pushed through the screen door.

Madam Gautier leaned toward the door. "And while you're in the kitchen, bring the pitcher of lemonade from the fridge and four glasses."

"Yes, ma'am," Lissette called out from inside the house.

"She always brings me eclairs when she wants something," Madam Gautier whispered. "It used to be a potion or elixir to cure her broken heart. I've made more than a dozen of those for her since she turned eleven. Lately, she wants more than elixirs for a broken heart. She wants me to teach her everything I know about Voodoo and magic."

Holly frowned. "Is that a good idea? I know she's family and all, but she's always been one for stirring up trouble."

Her grandmother patted her arm. "Not to worry, my dear. I've only taught her a few spells to make her laundry smell better. I also showed her how to make salves to ease wounds and pain. I won't give her secrets that could cause others pain."

"Gran, you're a wise and powerful Voodoo queen." Holly gave her grandmother a quick hug and then stepped back against Simon's hand. "I'm not one to tell you who you can or cannot teach all you know. I only hope the ones you teach use the magic for good."

Holly glanced toward the door. "Shh. She doesn't need to hear us talking about the merits of teaching her all there is to know about Voodoo. She can be as catty and vindictive as any mean girl in high school, or blindly reckless with her own abilities or of other people's feelings."

Her grandmother nodded. "I'd hate to think of what might happen if she were set loose with even half of the more powerful tools in the Voodoo spell and incantations playbook. The entire town of Bayou Mambaloa would be at risk."

The old woman sighed. "Still, she is a Gautier and my granddaughter."

"And my cousin," Holly added.

Madam Gautier nodded. "Family."

Holly nodded. "Only good and beneficial spells for that one."

"At least until she grows out of her selfish ways. I believe she will one day."

Holly smiled "You are ever the optimist."

"Now that you're back, you should join me and Gisele. I'm teaching her everything. She has a good heart, that one. As do you."

"You'll show me all the good spells and potions?"

"And some of the not-so-nice ones," her grandmother winked. "Some folks need a little reminder to be nice. I can teach you how to give a miscreant a case of jock itch."

Simon frowned. "You can do that?"

Holly laughed, and her grandmother joined in, the sound warm and joyful.

At that moment, Lissette stepped out on the porch carrying a tray with the pitcher of lemonade and four glasses. "What's so funny?"

"Jock itch," her grandmother answered, and laughed again.

Holly stepped forward and lifted the heavy glass pitcher from the tray, while Lissette set everything

SIMON

else on a table. She poured tangy liquid into each glass.

As she filled the glasses, Lissette passed one to her grandmother and the second to Simon, smiling up at him with her big, beautiful brown eyes.

Holly glanced up just as her cousin batted her eyes at Simon.

Not that Simon was interested in her dark-haired cousin in the least.

Holly's cheeks flushed pink, and her eyes flashed.

Lissette batted her eyes at Simon again and then turned to face Holly. "I heard a rumor that you and Simon are officially together. I heard another rumor that you hired him as a bodyguard. Which one is it, pray tell?"

Holly shoved a glass of lemonade into Lissette's hand. Holding her own, she stepped between Simon on Lissette and smiled up at Simon.

Yeah, it was tight. Probably forced. But it was a smile.

"The first rumor is the one to go with. The second one is a lucky bonus of having a boyfriend who doubles as a bodyguard." She leaned up on her toes and brushed a kiss across his cheek. "Isn't that right, sweetheart?"

He wanted to laugh at her attempt at making them appear to be a couple. Instead, he wrapped his free arm around her, pulled her closer and planted a kiss on her startled lips. "That's right, babe." He shot a grin toward Lissette. "Holly's my little bundle of love."

Lissette's eyes narrowed. She took a sip of her lemonade and swallowed before she asked. "What brings you two out to see Mémère?"

"That's between me and Mémère," Holly said.

"You're here because of the curse, aren't you?" Lissette's eyes widened, and she turned to her grandmother. "I'd like to be here when you make the spell or potion to undue Holly's curse. Please say you'll show me, too."

Madam Gautier's brow furrowed. "I haven't said I'd help her yet. I'm not entirely certain I can."

"Of course you can," Lissette argued. "You're Madam Gautier, Bayou Mambaloa's Voodoo queen."

The old woman shook her head. "That doesn't mean I can do anything and everything. Some things are beyond my control." She nodded toward Holly. "This might be one of them."

Holly's shoulders slumped. "Really? If you can't help me, how will I break the curse?"

Her grandmother stared into her glass of lemonade. "I'll have to think about it and look through my books and notes. It could take time."

"Mémère, I might not have time," Holly said softly. "I've had two messages. That's more than Paul and my parents had before..."

Madam Gautier patted Holly's arm. "I know, dear.

I can't predict your future, to know if you are truly in danger, but I know someone who might."

Holly frowned. "I'd rather work with you, Mémère."

"I need more time. While you're waiting, go see Lady LaChance, the nutria seer over in Bayou Miste. She might be able to tell you if you are in danger."

"Nutria seer?" Simon asked.

"Lady LaChance communes with a nutria to predict the future." Madam Gautier waved a hand. "Much like a fortune teller who reads tarot cards. I've heard she's had significant success."

Holly's brow twisted. "I don't know, Mémère."

"Go. See her. By the time you come back, I should know more."

"What is a nutria?" Simon asked.

Lissette snorted softly. "An animal. You think an animal can predict whether or not Holly is in danger?"

Simon was positive an animal couldn't predict whether Holly was in danger. They didn't need to know whether or not she was. Based on the threatening messages and her losses of the past, Simon was one-hundred-percent sure Holly was in danger. He didn't need a woman to commune with a nutria to tell him that.

Madam Gautier gave Lissette what Simon would classify as the stink-eye. "Holly will go to Lady LaChance. I will work on identifying the curse and come up with a cure, if there is one to be had." She lifted her chin.

"If you work a cure, will you at least let me watch?" Lissette asked.

Holly tensed beside Simon.

"My beautiful granddaughter," Madam Gautier cupped Lissette's cheek. "When you show me that you care about anyone besides yourself, I might consider teaching you what I know."

Lissette's brow descended into a stormy frown. "I care about you." She flung her hand toward Holly. "I care about my cousins, even though they don't care about me. What? Do you want me to prove that I care about the whole damned bayou like you?" She lifted her chin. "Fine."

Simon knew when a woman said "fine," all was not fine. He stepped forward, placing his body a bit more between Holly and her cousin, and braced himself in case he had to dive in to save Madam Gautier.

Lissette's cheeks had turned a ruddy red, and her eyes glistened. "I'll show you who and what I care about. You'll see." She turned to Holly. "You all will see. I'm not just the afterthought granddaughter of the great Madam Gautier. Sure, I've made some bad decisions. Yes, I've made mistakes. I don't know anyone who hasn't, but I've learned that I'm a strong, independent woman who doesn't need her family's approval. I'll make it on my own. I'll show you."

Lissette turned away and descended the steps without looking back.

Holly started to follow her cousin. "Lissette."

Her grandmother caught her arm. "Let her go," she said softly.

"But I have to go after her," Holly said, tears welling in her eyes. "She's family. And we have so little family left."

Madam Gautier nodded. "She is family. But she thinks she has something to prove to the rest of us." Her head shook side to side. "That's where she's wrong. She has only to prove to herself what she just claimed."

Holly stared after her cousin. "That she's a strong, independent woman who can make it on her own?"

"Yes." Her grandmother waved a hand toward Lissette as she slipped into the pirogue without tipping the boat or splashing water on her dress. "All of her broken hearts. All the trouble she has stirred up."

"She's always had to have a man in her life," Holly said softly, "and constantly demands attention."

"She needs to learn she can survive on her own, and that she doesn't need anyone but herself to make her happy. We will always be here for her. She has to be there for herself. She has to shine because she wants to shine for Lissette, and be happy because she chooses to be happy, not because she has to have someone to make her happy."

Holly pressed a hand to her chest. "But she looks so alone."

Simon watched the woman press the paddle against the shore and push the pirogue out into the water. Soon, she was cleaving the water, channeling her anger into the paddling away.

Like Holly, he wanted to go after the woman. To ease her pain and sense of rejection.

"What if she doesn't figure out that she is the only one who can make her life better?" Holly asked.

Her grandmother lifted her chin. "I predict she will figure it out sooner rather than later. She will risk all when the time comes, and gain everything for her sacrifice."

Holly stared at her grandmother, eyes narrowed. "I thought you said you couldn't predict the future."

"I said I couldn't predict *your* future. Go. See Lady LaChance. I have work to do." The older woman started gathering glasses.

Holly hurried to add glasses to the tray. "Let me help."

"I'm old, not helpless." Madam Gautier lifted the tray with the pitcher and glasses, paused and met her granddaughter's gaze. "I will do what I can to help. But don't rely solely on me. Seek the help of others. Voodoo isn't the only magic you should trust. There are a lot of smart people out there. Let them help."

"I will, Mémère," Holly promised. "I love you and our family. I don't want to lose anyone else."

"Then explore all possibilities." She turned with her loaded tray.

Simon got ahead of her to open the screen door.

"And you," the woman said, her brow creasing fiercely. "The only way to move on is to learn from the past but leave it in the past. Life is short. The thing is, you never know how short. It's best to live every day like it's your last. Grab for the joy now. Live. Now." She disappeared into the house, her words leaving him feeling as if she'd punched him in the gut.

He let the door close and stared at it without really seeing it. The past he relived every night in his dreams rushed through his mind like a movie on continuous replay. Only, this time, he mentally hit the stop button, not pause, where it froze on the image of Johnny dying in his arms.

Full stop, where the movie screen turned black, forcing him to look up and focus on the world around him.

Holly stood at his side, her brow creased, her eyes worried. "Are you all right?"

"How did she know?" he asked.

Holly touched his arm. "Mémère has a way of reading people. She can sense their pain when they aren't even aware they're harboring it. She can be brutally spot-on." Holly hooked her arm through his. "Come on. It's getting late. We need to get the skiff back to the marina before nightfall, and I have to go to work."

"Right." He squared his shoulders and shoved the Voodoo queen's words of wisdom to the back of his mind. For now.

Focusing on the world right there in front of him, he knew what he had to do.

Protect Holly.

The past wasn't going to do it for him. Johnny was gone. No amount of regret and wishing otherwise was going to bring him back.

He took her hand and started down the steps.

Holly shook free of his hand. "Go to the skiff without me," she said.

"I'm not leaving you," he said.

She smiled. "I know. But I have to release Napoleon."

Simon shook his head. "He'll attack."

"He'll attack you," Holly said. "He doesn't like men or males of any species. He sees them as a threat to his hens." She waved Simon away. "Go on. I'll be okay."

Simon reluctantly walked to the dock and climbed into the boat.

As soon as he was seated, Holly lowered the fishnet from the hook on the post and flipped it over.

The rooster dropped to the ground, shook out his feathers and then ran toward his hens.

Holly hung the net back on the post and grinned

as she strode down to the dock without being attacked by Napoleon, the killer rooster.

She dropped onto the back bench and fired up the outboard while Simon untied the line from the cleat.

Simon sat in silence, scanning the reeds, trees and brush flanking the channels as they wove through the bayou and emerged into the open, close to the marina.

Holly expertly guided the skiff up to the dock, cutting the engine in time to drift up to the boardwalk.

Simon tied the line to the piling just the way he'd found it and climbed onto the wooden decking. He reached back to help Holly up, but didn't let go until she was in his arms. He held her there for a moment, loving the feel of her body pressed to his, her grandmother's words echoing in his mind.

Live every day like it's your last...

Grab for the joy...

Holly looked up into his eyes. "Simon?"

He sighed, brushed his lips across her forehead and stepped back. "I like your grandmother."

Then he turned and led the way back to the marina building.

The marina owner and the high school principal stood at the edge of the dock. Joyce held a fishing pole in her hands. Mitchell was behind her, his arm around her, his hands over hers on the pole. Together, they leaned the pole back and then flicked it forward, unleashing the line with a hook and a bobber on the end.

The bobber plopped into the water several yards out.

Joyce laughed and smiled.

"See? You're a natural," Mitchell said. He caught sight of Simon and Holly and lowered his arms to his sides. "Look who's back," he said.

Joyce turned, her face radiant with a smile. "Did you see that, Holly? I'm learning how to cast."

"I saw." Holly grinned at her friend's excitement. "You did great."

"We just wanted you to know we're back and the skiff is also back where it belongs," Simon said.

"All is well with Madam Gautier?" Mitchell asked.

Holly nodded. "She's doing well. Feisty as ever."

Mitchell chuckled. "The woman tells it like it is."

"Tell me about it," Simon said, running a hand through his hair.

Mitchell laughed. "I swear she's a mind-reader. But she gives good advice and cures for what ails you." His gaze went to Joyce as she reeled in the bobber a little at a time.

"You wouldn't happen to know where we can find a Lady LaChance, would you?" Simon asked. "Madam Gautier said she's over in Bayou Miste."

Mitchell shook his head. "Can't say as I've run into her. If you want to know anything about Bayou

Miste, talk to your teammate, Beau Boyette. Half the people in that parish are Boyettes."

Simon nodded. "That's right. He might know where to find Lady LaChance."

"If he doesn't," Mitchell said, "I guarantee he has a family member over there that does."

"Thanks for the loan of your skiff," Holly said. "We might need it again soon."

"You're welcome to it anytime." Mitchell returned his attention to his student, the school principal, and threaded another worm on her hook.

Simon took Holly's hand and walked with her to the truck.

"No one's watching," she said. "You don't need to pretend we're together."

"I'm practicing," he lied. He didn't need practice to feel natural holding Holly's hand. It felt right, and he liked it.

Once in the truck, he turned to her. "Where to?"

She drew in a breath and let it out. "I don't have to be at work for another hour, and I just realized we completely missed lunch. How about the diner for a bite to eat?"

"I could eat a couple of burgers." He drove out of the parking lot onto the road into town.

"Principal Ashcraft and Mitchell appear to have hit it off," Holly said. "Joyce looked like a giddy teenager."

"They seemed to be having fun."

"Gives me hope."

"Hope for what?"

"Oh, I don't know..." She waved her hand, "Life, happiness...love. They aren't as young as they used to be. I know it's not Joyce's first time in a relationship. Given that her last one ended in divorce, I'm happy she's opening her heart for a second chance at finding happiness. She's proving that it's never too late for love."

Simon shot her a glance. "Do you still miss Paul?" he asked.

"I miss our friendship. I missed having someone to talk to in the evening. My time in Atlanta taught me to live alone. For the first few months, I was desperately lonely and depressed. After a while, I got tired of wallowing and found ways to battle my depression. I exercised, took up painting—though I'm not that good at it—and read a lot of books. Both fiction and nonfiction."

"Did it help?"

She nodded. "It did. Once I was past the depression and the grief of losing Paul and my parents had mellowed, I was able to look back at my relationship with Paul. We'd been friends since high school, but we never committed to marriage. I loved him. As a friend. I think we were both afraid of getting married and ruining our good friendship."

"Do you feel like you wasted all those years being

friends when you could've been looking for a different kind of love?" Simon asked.

"No. I think we were each other's safety net. Love can be messy and hard. It was easy being friends. We weren't ready to find that someone special we wanted to spend the rest of our lives with."

Simon remembered Johnny telling him about Lacy shortly after they'd met. He'd said it was love at first sight and that he was going to marry her.

Looking back, knowing what he knew and how things had worked out, Simon was glad Johnny had grabbed at happiness when he had. Like Madam Gautier had said, *Life is short. You don't know how short.*

Johnny had been happy with Lacy and over the moon when they'd had a son. Though his life had been cut short, he'd lived it to the fullest and loved with all his heart. Not just his small family, but also his teammates, his brothers in arms. Men he'd given his life for.

"What about you?" Holly asked. "Have you ever been in love?"

Simon snorted softly. "I thought I was once," he said. "But she chose bucktooth Bobby." His lips quirked. "We were nine years old."

Holly shook her head. "That doesn't count."

"It did back then."

"You really haven't ever found someone you wanted to spend your life with?"

"Really," he said. "I dated but never committed.

Being Delta Force wasn't easy on relationships. I felt like it would be setting up for failure."

"I have to admit I felt guilty that I didn't grieve overly long for Paul. Yes, I missed him, but I also felt like it freed me to be open to other possibilities."

"Like Cody West?" Simon poked.

She backhanded his arm, grinning. "Absolutely not." Her grin faded. "I also felt guilty that I didn't push hard enough for answers about his death. I don't think the sheriff's department dug deep enough. They said it was an accident. Granted, there were no indications otherwise. No one witnessed him having an argument earlier that day. No skid marks were found on the highway. He had no reason to commit suicide when he had a good job and a steady relationship."

Simon pulled up in front of the diner and shifted into park.

"Simon?" Holly sat staring at the diner in front of them. "I don't think law enforcement looked hard enough into Paul's death. And though they had multiple search parties looking for over a week for my parents' bodies, they never found them. Mémère made a good point. I need to ask for all the help I can get." She turned to face him. "If the offer is still open to enlist your computer guy's help, I accept. I've run from this long enough. I'll try everything in my power to end this curse, whether by magic or powered by people."

SIMON

Simon let out a sigh. "I'm glad you said that. Because, after you went to sleep last night, I lay awake for a while, worried that we weren't attacking your problem from all angles. I stepped out on the deck and made a call to Swede in Montana. I told him about the messages, about your parents and Paul. If I know Swede, he's been on it all day. Hopefully, he'll have some useful information for us soon." He held up his hand. "And we'll follow up with your grandmother's request to see the animal seer tomorrow. We should try anything that helps us get to the bottom of this."

CHAPTER 8

Normally, Holly would be mad at someone if he went behind her back to get more information. In this case, she was glad Simon had made the call. It meant his guy, Swede, was already searching for clues into the death of Paul and the disappearances of her parents.

Swede might not come up with any more than what law enforcement had, but she had to try. Finding her parents' bodies would almost be better than living forever, wondering if they were out there somewhere.

Almost.

Having them home would be the best scenario, but she wasn't getting her hopes up.

Work was hectic that night, with a New Orleans Saints game playing on the televisions mounted above the bar and in the corners of the dining area.

The crowd got loud whenever there was a touchdown or a bad call by the referees.

By the end of her shift, her ears were ringing and her feet ached from hurrying between tables to keep the beer and food flowing.

The one saving grace of the evening was Simon, perched on a barstool, alternately watching the game and her throughout the evening.

Rene hadn't squawked once about her bodyguard taking up space. He even comped his soft drinks and shared war stories. Holly hadn't realized Rene had served in the military. However, it appeared he loved it when members of the Brotherhood Protectors spent time at his bar. He reminisced about his days on active duty and thanked Simon and his team for their service.

When Cody came in halfway through her shift, Holly made a point of walking over to put her hand on Simon's shoulder.

He'd done one better by wrapping his arm around her waist and pulling her in for a quick hug.

Out of the corner of Holly's eye, she saw her former friend glare, turn and head for the other side of the room where Danny was serving customers.

Good. Holly didn't have the time or energy to fend off unwanted advances from him.

The game ended close to eleven o'clock, after going into overtime, with the Saints ultimately losing.

Disappointed, the crowd quickly dispersed, leaving the Crawdad Hole empty by midnight.

Holly and Danny quickly stacked chairs on the tables. While Holly swept, Danny mopped. Halfway through the room, Holly glanced up to find that Simon had found another broom and had started sweeping from the opposite side of the restaurant, working his way toward her. They finished quickly and dumped the contents of the dustpan in the garbage. Simon started for the storeroom but was intercepted by Rene, carrying another mop. When Simon began mopping from the other end of the room, Holly insisted on taking the mop from him. "You're doing your job. Let me do mine, or Rene will dock my pay."

Simon relinquished his hold on the mop and rejoined Rene at the bar, talking to the older man as he restocked the shelves and thoroughly cleaned every surface.

By the time they finished the floors, it was twelve thirty, and Holly was beyond tired and glad she didn't have to drive back to the houseboat.

She dragged herself up into the passenger seat of Simon's truck and leaned her head back. "There are advantages to having a bodyguard," she murmured. "I can let him drive, while I pass out."

"Close your eyes," he said. "I'll wake you when we get there."

"It's only a ten-minute drive." But she closed her eyes and was asleep before Simon left the parking lot.

The chirp of a cell phone brought her back to the surface to find they'd arrived at the houseboat.

The cell phone chirped again as Simon shifted into park. He grabbed the device from the cupholder and answered, "Whatcha got, Swede?"

Instantly awake, Holly sat up straighter and leaned toward Simon, hoping to hear what his computer guy had to say.

"Hold one," Simon said. "Holly's here with me. I'm going to put you on speaker."

He touched a button on his phone and said, "Shoot."

"Hi, Holly. Swede here. I did some digging on the death of your friend Paul Jameson, and I'm still working on the disappearances of your parents."

"What did you find?" Holly asked.

"Like I said, I'm still working on your parents, but I ran across an anomaly in the coroner's autopsy of Paul Jameson."

Holly leaned closer to the phone, her pulse quickening. "What kind of anomaly?"

"The sheriff's reports showed no signs of his vehicle being forced off the road or any evidence of tampering with the vehicle. Thus, they assumed Paul lost control, ran off the road and died when his vehicle submerged in the bayou."

"Yes?" Holly said. "That was all part of the report I

read. They called it an accident. What was the anomaly in the coroner's report?"

"There was no presence of any drugs, alcohol or toxins in his blood," Swede continued.

"I know that," Holly said, her patience thinning. "I read the coroner's report several times."

"What you might not have seen, because it was buried in the coroner's notes, was that there was no white, pink or foamy mixture in his airways," Swede said.

Holly frowned. "So?"

"And there was no water in his lungs."

Silence filled the cab of the pickup as those words sank into Holly's head.

"No water in his lungs?" She struggled to wrap her thoughts around that. "But he drowned. There should've been water in his lungs."

"Both the absence of that foamy mixture in his airways and the lack of water in his lungs make it clear," Swede paused for a moment, then added, "Paul didn't die from drowning."

"He died before he entered the water," Simon said.

"Why would the coroner report the cause of death as drowning?" Holly asked.

"I'd suggest you ask him yourself," Swede said. "Only you might be challenged to find him. He left his job as the parish medical examiner a couple of weeks following Paul's death. This was after he applied for and received a freshly minted passport. I searched through his now-defunct bank account records and found a charge for airfare to Cabo San Lucas, Mexico."

"Paul died before he ran into the bayou?" She shook her head. "Of what?"

"That, I can't tell you," Swede said. "There was no indication of heart failure and, like I said, no drugs, alcohol or poisons found in his blood. There are some toxins that are lethal that don't show up in blood and tissue analysis."

"Are you telling me Paul was..." Holly pressed a hand to her mouth, "murdered?"

"That would be my guess," Swede said. "Either the M.E. knew who did it or was paid to falsify that report by an anonymous donor and told to leave the country as soon as possible."

"Wow." The next thought that rushed into Holly's head made her press her knuckles to her lips to hold back a sob. She had to breathe in and out several times before he could speak past the lump in her throat. "If Paul was murdered...that means that my parents' boat accident might not have been an accident at all."

Her stomach roiled. Suddenly, the truck cab seemed to close in around her. Her heart raced, and she couldn't seem to get enough air into her lungs.

Holly shoved open her door and slid out of her seat. When her feet hit the ground, her knees buckled, and she sank to the dirt. Once there, she curled into the fetal position, her body spasming with the force of her sobs.

Hands gripped her arms and pulled her up against a hard wall of muscles. Arms wrapped around her and held her close, rocking her gently as the grief she'd refused to acknowledge and the hope she'd clung to for the past six months dissolved into a messy, horrible truth she wasn't ready to grasp.

Through her sobs, Simon's voice droned in a continuous, soothing tone, promising she would be all right, telling her he was there for her and wouldn't let go.

She cried until there were no more tears left inside, and she succumbed to a numbness she couldn't push past.

Simon scooped her up in his arms and rose.

Holly couldn't even manage to raise her arm to loop it over his shoulder. She closed her eyes to the starlight twinkling cheerfully overhead. Did they ever grieve?

He carried her down to the dock and across the gangway, shifting her gently to maneuver the key in the lock. Then he was through the door with her, kicking it shut behind him.

He didn't stop there.

Barely aware of her surroundings, Holly rested her cheek against Simon's chest. The beat of his heart was like a metronome. She focused on its steady rhythm, letting it cloak her thoughts against the horrible truth.

Paul and her parents had been murdered.

Another sob rose up her throat. She turned her head and buried her face in Simon's chest, muffling the sound of her grief.

Then they were going up, slowly, step by step, her feet bumping against the wall.

Simon stopped, leaned over and laid her on a soft surface, her head coming to rest on a pillow.

When his arms drew away from her, panic set in. The muscles she hadn't been able to move moments ago suddenly worked. She flung her arms around Simon's neck and held on with all her might. "Don't," she croaked from a throat ravaged by her sobs. "Please. Don't leave."

Simon froze for a moment and then said. "Sweetheart, I promise I won't leave you, but give me a minute to breathe." After he eased her arms from around his neck, he removed her shoes, kicked off his own and lay on the bed beside her.

Then he gathered her in his arms, pulling her close.

Holly rested her cheek against his chest again, eager to listen to the calming beat of his heart, pushing the truth to the back of her mind if only for the night. She needed time to assimilate the data and accept it. Just not tonight.

Simon's hand stroked her hair, smoothing it back

from her forehead.

Holly closed her eyes.

"Sleep, sweetheart," his deep voice whispered against her cheek. Warm lips pressed gently against her forehead.

"You'll stay?" she asked, her lips moving against his T-shirt.

"As long as you like," he promised.

Secure in Simon's arms, Holly disappeared into a deep, dark abyss where pain couldn't follow, where numbness reigned and grief could damn well wait.

SIMON HELD Holly well into the night, even after his arms went numb. Her tortured expression upon learning her parents might have been murdered was bad enough. Finding her curled into the fetal position on the ground had broken his heart.

He'd wanted to take her pain away, knowing he couldn't. Instead, he'd done the only thing he could to help her. He'd held her close, rocking her gently, speaking to her in whispers, assuring her that she'd be all right when he wasn't certain she ever would.

When her sobs had died away, he'd carried her into the houseboat and up to her bed. Though he hadn't planned on staying, he couldn't leave her. Not when she'd begged him to stay.

The problem was that he was afraid to go to sleep,

afraid his own nightmares would turn violent and that he might hurt Holly without realizing it.

He lay awake as long as he could, and eventually, closed his eyes.

Just for a moment.

He knew he was back in a dream. Knew it wasn't real, but he could sense the heat, smell the dust and feel Johnny dying in his arms.

"No," he whispered, his heart pounding while his friend's slowed. "Don't die."

No matter how many times he relived that night, he couldn't change the outcome.

Johnny would give him the lucky rabbit's foot, speak of his love for his wife and son and then die.

Only this time was different. Right before Johnny succumbed to his injuries, his hand tightened in Simon's. "Buddy, I'm dying. Not you. You must live every day like it's your last... Grab for the joy..."

Johnny's face morphed into that of a withered old woman with fierce eyes.

Madam Gautier.

When she spoke, her words echoed all around him, "Live. Now."

HANDS SMOOTHED OVER HIS CHEST. Fingers slipped

beneath the hem of his shirt and flattened against his bare skin.

A gentle female voice whispered against his ear. "Just a dream."

He raised his hand to cover the one on his chest, the fabric of his shirt between them.

"This feels so real," he murmured.

"You're here now. With me," she said. "Not in a dream."

He opened his eyes to muted starlight shining through windows. The air wasn't thick with debris. He drew in a deep breath. Instead of the dry scent of an arid landscape, he inhaled the pleasant bouquet of flowers. Turning his head, something tickled his nose. A feather? He leaned into it.

Not a feather.

Hair...thick curls lying in wild disarray across a clean white pillow.

Eyes stared into his.

"Hey," Holly said, a gentle smile curving her lips. "You're back." The hand on his chest disappeared and found its way to his cheek. "Are you okay?"

He nodded.

"Bad dream?" she asked as she brushed her slender thumb over his jawline.

"Johnny died," he stated.

She nodded. "You couldn't change it, could you?"

"No. However, this time, his final words were

different. Then it wasn't Johnny, it was Madam Gautier telling me to live now."

Holly's soft laughter warmed his heart and the skin closest to her lips. "Must have been a helluva nightmare."

His arm tightened around her, and he pulled her close. "No. Johnny said he was dying. Knew he wouldn't make it, but he wanted me to live."

Her hand smoothed down his neck to rest on his chest, her fingers curling into the soft jersey of his T-shirt. "He was a good friend," she said.

"The best," Simon said. Then, he pushed back the residuals of his dream and studied Holly's face. "What about you? Do you feel any better?"

She nodded. "Much better. Thanks for being here." Her hand moved across his chest and lower to slip under his shirt again. "For staying."

She lay curled into his side, her calf draped over his thigh, her sex pressing into his hip.

Simon's groin tightened. He caught her hand through the shirt. "If you're okay, I'll head down to the couch."

Holly stiffened. "You don't have to go if you don't want to," she whispered so softly, he had to lean his head closer to hear.

"Stay," she said, the word lighter than air, her breath warm on his neck.

"It's not my job to sleep with you."

"If you weren't my bodyguard, would you stay?"

she asked, her fingers curling into the hairs on his chest, her nails scraping softly across his skin. "Do you want to stay?"

His hand tightened around hers. "Yes," he admitted. "But I can't."

"Or won't?"

"I can't stay and not...touch you." He let go of her hand and slid his across her arm to her hip, pulling her closer, gently grinding her sex against his body.

Her leg swept higher, her knee nudging against the bulge in his jeans. "What if I want to touch you?"

Simon groaned.

If she continued on that path, doing the things she was doing, he'd be in serious pain from the unforgiving stiffness of denim.

"Sweetheart, I'd let you touch every inch of my body—as much or as little as you like."

Her fingers drifted lower to cup his junk, squeezing gently.

Again, he covered her hand with his, halting her attack on his senses. "Don't go there if you don't want to go all the way. Once we start, I can't guarantee I'll be able to stop. You're doing crazy things to my control."

"Then let go of that control," she whispered against his neck. "Touch me. Hold me. Make love to me."

"You're my client," he said as a last-ditch effort to stop what was building between them. "Isn't there something in the playbook...a rule that states you don't make love with the client?"

"Fuck the rule book." Holly leaned up on her elbow and stared down into his face, her eyes dark pools in the gloom. "If you don't want to make love to me, just say it. I'll go sleep on the couch."

When he didn't answer right away, she swung her legs over the side of the bed and pushed to her feet.

Simon snagged her arm and yanked her back. She landed on the bed beside him and immediately tried to rise again.

He held onto her arm, anchoring her to the bed and to him.

"Let go," she said. "You obviously have no desire to make love with me. Forget it."

"Stay," he said. "I want to make love to you."

She shook her head. "I don't need your pity fuck. I can pleasure myself. I know my own body and my sweet spots better than any man."

Again, she tried to get up. He tugged her back down.

Her sass and anger only made Simon more determined to keep her there. His brain told him to let her go before he lost himself in her.

He asked himself if that would be a bad thing and decided he didn't care.

"I'm intrigued by your body and sweet spots." He sat up behind her, brushed her hair off her neck and pressed his lips to the spot right under her earlobe.

Holly sucked in a sharp breath and let it out on a soft moan.

"If I promise this isn't a pity fuck, will you show me what pleases you most? I'm a quick study."

"I'm sure you are," she said, her voice breathy as if she couldn't quite get enough air.

He touched his hand to her shoulder and slid it down her arm to her waist, then back up, brushing his palm ever so slightly against the swell of her breast.

"Interested?" he whispered against her ear.

"Mildly," she said, her tone dry.

He cupped her breast in his hand and squeezed gently. "This could be so much better... skin to skin." With his other hand, he tilted her head toward him and pressed his lips to her temple. All the while, he pinched her nipple between his thumb and forefinger. Even through the fabrics of her shirt and bra, he could feel the tip form a hard little button.

His pulse thickened and quickened, pushing heat and adrenaline throughout his body to pool in his groin.

Holly leaned her head back against his shoulder, her chest rising and falling with each labored breath. She raised her hand and took the one he had on her breast.

For a moment, he froze, expecting her to stop him. Instead, she guided him lower to the hem of her shirt and under it.

The warmth of her skin against his palm sent fire through his system. He went back to the breast he'd fondled, cupped it and squeezed gently.

It wasn't enough for him.

Or for her.

In an impatient move, she leaned away from him, yanked her shirt up and over her head and flung it away. Then she reached behind her back and fumbled with the hooks on her bra.

Simon brushed aside her attempts and expertly freed the hooks and slid the straps down her arms.

Once free of her top, Holly spun and helped Simon out of his shirt, then reached for the button on his jeans.

In a scramble of knees and elbows, they shed their remaining clothes and collapsed against the mattress, naked and slightly breathless.

Simon chuckled, pulled Holly into his arms and kissed her hard. When his tongue slid over the seam of her lips, she opened to him, her hand weaving into the hair at the back of his neck, urging him closer, deeper.

Rolling Holly onto her back, Simon settled over her and bent to capture her earlobe between his teeth, nipping gently. "Is this one of your sweet spots?"

She shook her head. "Lower."

Up for the challenge, he kissed a path from her chin downward, tasting every inch of her. He paused to suck her breast into his mouth, flicking the hardened tip several times. "Is this a sweet spot?" he asked.

"Yes!" she breathed.

He moved to the other side and sucked that nipple into his mouth.

Holly's back arched, pressing her breast deeper, a moan rumbling in her throat.

He moved lower, leading with his hands, his mouth following, blazing a trail across her ribs. When he reached the juncture of her thighs, he cupped her sex and paused, desire welling up so fast and intensely he could barely breathe. "And this?" he asked, dipping his finger into her channel.

"Oh, yes." She drew her knees up and let them fall to the side, opening to him, allowing him full access.

Simon pressed a kiss to her folds as he slid a finger into her slick channel, swirled in her heat and added another. With his thumbs, he parted those folds and flicked his tongue across her clit.

Holly gasped and bucked, her hips rising off the bed, her body tensing. "That's the spot. There."

When he did it again, she grasped his head, sinking her fingers into his hair to hold him there. "Again," she rasped.

With slow, deliberate strokes, he played her sex, teasing that nubbin of flesh again and again until she rocked beneath him, whimpering softly, begging him to keep going.

For a moment, he abandoned her clit and slipped his tongue into her channel, tasting her juices before coming back to the center of her pleasure.

Simon stroked and flicked in a steadily increasing rhythm until Holly's heels dug into the mattress and her ass rose off the bed, her entire body stiff as she teetered on the edge of her release. Then she moved, her hips pumping, her hands tugging and pulling his hair with each wave of her orgasm.

When she collapsed against the mattress, Simon climbed up her body and kissed her lips. "Had enough?" he asked.

Her eyes widened, and her hands slid down his back to cup his ass. "Not nearly." Then she pressed him closer until his cock nudged her entrance.

He held back, testing her channel with tentative dips, making sure she was ready to take all of him.

Poised at her entrance, her hands pressing hard, urging him to take her, he remembered...

"Hold that thought." He bent, pressed a kiss to her lips and then rolled off the bed and searched frantically for his jeans and the wallet in the back pocket.

"Are you kidding?" she wailed. "You can't stop now."

Simon let out a relieved chuckle when he found what he was looking for and dug the sole condom out.

With the packet in hand, he returned to her, knelt

between her legs and rolled the condom over his engorged shaft.

Holly gripped his cock and guided him to her.

Determined to take it slow and let her adjust to his size, Simon eased in.

Holly had other ideas. She gripped his buttocks firmly and brought him home in one swift, fluid yank.

Fully sheathed, he inhaled and exhaled several times and then moved. With her hands on his ass, urging him to go faster, he pressed in and out, increasing speed as his control slipped and primal instinct took over.

Soon, he was hammering into her, his body tensing, quickly approaching the edge.

Holly raised her hips to meet his thrusts again and again, writhing against the sheets, her hair in a wild halo around her face. She was beautiful, unbound and giving freely without constraint.

Simon's orgasm rushed up inside him and burst forth like the finale of a pyrotechnic show. Wave after wave of impulses stormed free, shaking him to his very core as his cock pulsed inside her.

He didn't move, didn't breathe, the feeling so complete, he couldn't imagine anything that could compete.

When at last he was forced to fill his lungs or die, he dropped down, gathered her in his arms and kissed her.

Then he buried his face against her neck and sighed. "Wow."

"Yeah," she whispered. "Wow."

He rolled to his side and pulled her close, resting his hand on her naked hip.

For a long time, they lay still, in what felt like a kind of stunned silence.

"I didn't expect that," Holly finally said.

Simon tensed. "Expect what?"

"That level of intensity," she said.

He frowned and rose on his elbow. "Did I hurt you?"

She shook her head. "No. But I admit I'm a little scared."

Her words hit him square in the gut. "Oh, sweetheart, I should've taken it slower." He brushed his thumb over her cheek. "I didn't mean to scare you."

She captured his hand in hers and pressed her cheek into his palm. "You didn't scare me. What we did scared me."

"We don't have to do it again. I promise not to touch you if you don't want me to."

She laughed. "Oh, I want you to touch me. It's just…" she rolled toward him in the muted starlight, her skin painted blue by the night, her eyes dark, unreadable pools, "that was so incredible, I'm afraid… afraid it can't be duplicated. What if we peaked? What if we can't recapture that kind of perfection?

SIMON

What if from here on out we're doomed to mediocre sex?" She buried her face against his chest.

Simon stared down at her head, taking in her words, trying to understand their meaning.

A muffled snort shook her body against him. Then a giggle rocked her even more.

Determined to get to the bottom of things, he tipped her face up to his. "Woman, you slay me." He pressed a kiss to her forehead. "Sex between us..." another kiss to each of her eyelids, "could never..." one to the tip of her nose, "be anything but..." finally his lips settled on hers, "extraordinary."

She wrapped her hands around the back of his head and brushed her lips across his. "We'll have to test that theory."

He sighed and slid back into her. "Gladly."

They made love into the night, rocking the boat with their enthusiasm. Although some of the rocking might have been due to the wind that had spun up.

Eventually, Holly fell asleep in Simon's arms.

He held her, afraid to drift off. Afraid the night had been a fluke and that when he woke, it would all have been a dream.

At least it would have been a good dream, not the recurring nightmare of losing Johnny.

Perhaps he was moving past the PTSD that had plagued him for so long. Maybe being with Holly was good for him.

All he knew was that he didn't want the night to end.

CHAPTER 9

Bright light pressed against Holly's eyelids, forcing her to open them and blink.

Sunlight streamed in through the bedroom windows, a definitive indication that it was morning.

Having stayed up through most of the night, she groaned, pulled her pillow over her head and tried to go back to sleep.

Events of the night before flooded her thoughts, bringing her fully awake and aware of the warm body taking up more than half the bed beside her.

She shoved the pillow aside, rolled onto her side and stared at the man who'd absolutely ruined her. Well, ruined her for sex with anyone else ever again.

She drank her fill of his gorgeous face and sexy body while he slept peacefully. She loved the shadow of his beard that had scraped deliciously along her inner thighs as he'd gone down on her during the wee hours of the morning. When the sky had remained dark, fireworks had lit her world in the small bedroom.

Her pulse quickened. Was it too soon to wake him and ask for a repeat? She didn't want him to think she was needy.

But she was. Now that they'd taken things to the next level, she couldn't seem to get enough.

The next level.

What exactly was that level? Lust? Sex without commitment? Was there any hope of a level beyond the purely physical stage?

Neither one of them had promised anything. With things as uncertain as they were, it would be foolish to entertain the idea of a future together. Not to mention, they barely knew each other.

How long did someone need to know someone else before she knew he was the one?

And if Simon was her one, would that certainty only be on her side? What if she wasn't his one?

Throw in the potential curse she was carrying around with her, and he might not survive for her to find out if she was his one. Was he doomed because of the fake relationship they'd led everyone to believe?

"Why are you frowning?" Simon whispered.

While she'd been running increasingly disastrous scenarios through her head, Simon had opened his eyes and was now staring at her.

SIMON

"We shouldn't have told everyone you're my boyfriend," she blurted as she rolled out of the bed, pulled a T-shirt over her head and stood at the window.

"Too late. It's a small town. By now, we're practically married. We're even house hunting together." Simon sat up. "Why? What brought that up?"

"Paul was murdered. And my parents..." She swallowed hard on a sob, forcing it back. Crying wouldn't bring them back. "Whoever did that might come after you next."

"I'll take my chances," Simon said and came to stand behind her, his arms encircling her belly. "They might not have known what was coming. We have the advantage now because we're looking for something to happen."

Holly stared out at the bayou. "Something isn't right," she murmured.

"A lot isn't right. But we're going to figure this out. Swede's working on it from his end. We need to go find people close to what happened and ask the right questions."

Holly raised her hand. "No. Something isn't right with the view."

"What do you mean?"

Holly pulled on her jeans from the night before and darted for the stairs.

Simon rammed his legs into his jeans and hurried after her. "Slow down."

She didn't stop until she reached the door and flung it open.

The gangway was there. The dock wasn't. In fact, it was nowhere in sight.

Simon came to a halt behind her. "What the hell?"

Holly snorted. "The houseboat broke free of its mooring. That wind we felt last night must've pushed us out into the bayou—way out."

"Can't we fire up the engines and drive it back?"

Holly shook her head. "They don't work. The owners said they haven't worked for years. They never intended to move the boat."

Simon went back up the stairs and came back down with his cell phone.

"Who are you calling?" Holly asked.

"Mitchell at the marina."

Holly nodded.

Simon held the phone to his ear for longer than Holly thought necessary. Ultimately, he lowered the phone, a frown creasing his brow. "He isn't answering."

"Mitch can be really busy early in the morning, getting fishermen outfitted for their day on the bayou. We might have to wait a bit to try again."

Simon glanced at his phone. "We're supposed to meet with the realtor at ten, and then we were supposed to drive over to Bayou Miste to see your grandmother's nutria seer."

Holly shook her head. "We might need to call and postpone on all counts."

"How the hell does a houseboat break loose of its mooring?" Simon asked. He stepped back out on the deck, looked right and left, and back to the right, before taking off in that direction.

Holly watched as he lifted something, let it drop and then passed in front of her to inspect the other end of the boat in the same way. Holly joined him at that end of the houseboat. Simon held up a neatly cut length of rope, his mouth pressed in a thin line. "Someone cut the lines."

"Wouldn't we have heard it?" Holly asked.

Simon's lips twisted. "We were busy."

"Those aren't small lines. Surely, they would've had to saw through them. It's not like they could have used scissors to cut them. It would've taken time."

"Bolt cutters?" Simon suggested.

"Would bolt cutters work on rope and make a clean cut like that?" She shook her head. "I never thought to check the lines mooring the boat to the dock. Could they have cut them while we were away?"

Simon nodded. "That's a possibility."

"Why?"

"A threat? Or warning?"

"It's not like we're at risk of dying out here," Holly waved a hand. "Sooner or later, someone would come along and tow us back to the dock."

An explosion ripped through the air. The boat shook with enough force Holly fell to her knees and held on while the houseboat rocked in the water.

Moments later, smoke rose from the rear of the houseboat.

"Fire!" Holly shouted.

"Where's the fire extinguisher?" Simon asked.

"Attached to the wall in the kitchen," Holly said. "I'll get it."

She ran into the houseboat, heading straight for the extinguisher mounted on the wall. The bracket that held it was there, but the extinguisher was gone. She spent a few precious seconds looking for it, thinking the explosion had knocked it from its holding. When she couldn't find it, she grabbed a folded quilt off the back of the couch and ran back out on the deck.

Simon had found a hose on the deck. Thankfully, the water pump ran on a generator that kicked in when the electricity went out. Simon aimed the hose at the source of the fire on the back patio, though the narrow stream did little to extinguish the growing flame.

Holly ran past Simon and threw the quilted blanket onto the fire.

Simon aimed the hose at the blanket, soaking the fabric before the fire could consume it. In a few minutes of applying water to the blanket, the flames were effectively smothered, keeping them from spreading further.

Standing with the hose in one hand, still pouring water over the blanket, Simon spread his other arm wide.

Holly leaned into him, taking refuge in his embrace. "Okay then," she said. "That was a bit more than a warning."

Simon glanced past the deck to the bayou beyond. "Had the fire spread, we would've had to abandon the houseboat."

Holly stared at the reeds not far from where the houseboat had drifted. "See the brown pile of dead grass between the green marsh grass?"

Simon nodded.

"Look closer," Holly pointed. "See something dark moving between the nest and us? Looks like a log floating on the surface?"

Again, Simon nodded. "Is that what I think it is?"

She nodded. "It's a mama alligator, and that's her nest. They're extremely protective of their eggs and young."

"It's a good thing we were able to put out the fire," Simon said. "I'm a good swimmer but..."

"Not as good as she is." Holly drew in a deep breath and let it out slowly, wondering how long it would be before they'd get someone out to tow them back to the dock.

"Ahoy, there," a voice called out.

Holly looked out at the shadows of the morning bayou and spotted a boat floating nearby with a grizzled older man holding the handle of the till.

"J.D.?" she called out.

"That's me," the old man called out. "J.D. LaDue at your service." He tipped his fisherman's hat and bowed his head. "That you, Holly?"

Holly leaned over the rail. "Yes, it is."

"Aren't you a little far out in the bayou in that thing?" J.D. pointed a finger at the houseboat.

Holly gave the older man a crooked smile. "Hadn't planned on a morning tour. Someone cut the mooring lines."

J.D.'s bushy white eyebrows winged upward. "Ya don't say." He shook his head. "What's the world comin' to?"

Holly bit back an impatient comment and smiled at the man who understood the bayou like no other. "We could use a little help getting the houseboat back to the dock. Think you could let Mitchell Marceau know we're out here, drifting?"

J.D. lifted his chin. "I can do better than that." He turned his boat toward the houseboat. "I can get you back. Won't take long."

Holly frowned. "You think your little boat will tow this big ol' girl all the way back?"

J.D. patted the outboard engine. "This here is the little engine that could," he declared. "Toss me a line."

Simon leaned close to Holly. "Does he really think

that little boat of his can tow this massive house on pontoons?"

Holly shrugged. "J.D. has been a fixture in the bayou since before I can remember. If he says he can tow us, I'm sure he can." She hurried to the front of the houseboat and found a line long enough to reach J.D.'s boat. After tying it to a cleat on the bow, she tossed the other end of the line to J.D.

He missed the catch.

Holly gathered the line in.

Simon held out his hands. "Let me."

Holly handed the rope to Simon and stood back.

Simon whirled the line like a lasso several times before he released his hold. The line landed in front of J.D.

The old man grabbed the end, tied it to the rear of his skiff and lifted his chin toward Simon and Holly. "Ready?"

"Yes, sir," Simon responded.

J.D. turned his skiff and slowly drew the line taut. Then he eased his little boat forward, dragging the houseboat in its wake.

"Keep trying to reach Mitchell," Holly said. "At this rate, we might not get back to the dock until sometime next week."

Simon called Mitch several times over the hour-and-a-half it took J.D. to tow the houseboat back to its dock.

Simon spent the time cooking scrambled eggs and

bacon, saving back a paper plate full for J.D. for when they finally made it back to where they'd started the night before.

As they approached the dock, J.D. parked his skiff on the other side, took the lead line and walked with it up to the post that had been the anchor for the houseboat for a number of years.

He held up the cut line, his bushy white eyebrows forming a V over his nose. "This line has been cut."

Simon adjusted the gangway, lining it up with the dock before he stepped across and joined J.D.

Holly followed him to reaffirm that the houseboat's voyage into the bayou hadn't been an accident.

Back on land, Simon called 911 and reported the vandalism and the explosion that could have caused a conflagration sufficient to consume the houseboat and force Simon and Holly to abandon ship in the middle of the alligator-infested bayou. He called Remy to bring him up to date as well.

Deputy Shelby Taylor showed up to take their statements. The fire chief arrived shortly after and collected evidence he would have analyzed.

Though they couldn't state the obvious until the results came in, the sheriff and the police chief were convinced someone had tried to kill Holly and Simon.

Once they had the houseboat secure and their statements taken, Simon helped Holly up into his truck.

"You sure you want to go see the nutria seer and go house hunting after all that has happened this morning?" Holly asked.

"LaShawda has a few homes for us to tour," Simon said as he drove out onto the road and turned toward town. "Afterward, we can have lunch at the diner and decide whether or not we want to stay at the houseboat tonight or hole up in the boarding house. At least it won't float out into the bayou where alligator mamas are guarding their nests."

Holly's lips twitched. "That bothered you, didn't it?"

He shot a glance her way. "It didn't bother you?"

She shrugged. "Maybe for a moment when the fire flared up, but we put it out pretty quickly and didn't have to abandon ship."

Simon shook his head. "I don't like it," he said. "That was too close. If I hadn't been so preoccupied, I might've caught on to the sabotage sooner." He drew in a breath and let it out slowly. "What happened last night...though amazing... made me forget why I'm here in the first place." He shot a glance her way. "To protect you." Simon's lips pressed into a thin line. "I failed when I surrendered to my desire."

Holly sensed what he would say next and braced herself.

"Until this—whatever it is that's happening— is resolved, I can't lose focus." He stared straight ahead.

Holly's heart sank into the pit of her belly. "Which

means we won't be making love again," she stated softly. As badly as it hurt to say it, she was convinced it was the right thing to do. Whoever was after her and her loved ones might now target Simon.

"You're right," Holly said. "We can't be intimate. It puts you at risk and makes us lose focus on finding the source of the troubles."

Simon reached across the console, clasped her hand and brought it to his lips. "When whatever is happening is resolved, we can reconnect. Reevaluate." He met her gaze briefly across the console. "I'm not giving up on us. Not after last night."

"I'm not holding you to it," Holly said. "People do crazy things under stress. We might change our minds or discover that we don't have as much in common as we think we do. We might realize we have different needs and desires after all is said and done."

His lips twisted. "You're really killing my buzz." He gave her a tight smile and squeezed her hand before he let go. "I know what I want and desire. I want and desire you."

Holly's chest swelled with longing and something she suspected could be love, though she wasn't ready to admit it aloud. They had to overcome so much more before they could launch into the selfish pursuit of anything resembling commitment.

No, Simon hadn't declared his love for her. And why would he? They hadn't known each other long enough to know. Yeah, the sex had been mind-blowing. But was that enough?

Why was she even contemplating a future with the Brotherhood Protector who had only stuck around because it was his job to protect her?

He had no obligation to do anything else. He wasn't required to love her.

SIMON'S JAW CLENCHED. They'd had a close call that morning. He couldn't let things get away from him like they had. All because he'd made love to Holly.

If he fell in love with Holly, it was all on him. Not the job. He couldn't afford to fall in love. Couldn't afford to lose focus. Protecting Holly was what he had to do. And he'd nearly failed. Had they not extinguished the fire...

His gut knotted. He should have been on top of everything. Should have seen the lines had been cut. Should have felt the shift and sway of the houseboat moving away from the dock and out into the bayou. And he should have inspected every inch for explosives or incendiary devices.

Simon's cell phone chirped. He slowed his truck and pulled the phone from his pocket. "It's Swede." He answered the call. "Glad you called. We've had another incident."

"Tell me about it," Swede said.

Simon filled him in.

"I'll let Hank know what's going on," Swede said. "I also have some news for you."

"Yeah?" Simon set the phone on speaker. "Go ahead, you're on speaker. I'm with Holly."

"I did some more digging into Holly's parents, Bastian and Evangeline Gautier. They were environmental scientists, yes?"

"That's right," Holly answered. "They worked in the bayou. It was their passion to protect the ecosystem."

"Their names came up as employed by BioEnergen, a company in research and development of biological energy solutions."

Holly frowned. "No. They were working for the Bayou Resilience Project."

"I did find something about a non-profit by that name whose mission statement is to protect and preserve the bayous. More specifically, to stop harmful industrial practices, chemical runoff, and violations of environmental law."

"That's right," Holly said. "They were trying to come up with ways to encourage corporations to join the fight to preserve."

"It appears that the Bayou Resilience Project was a cover corporation for BioEnergen. A year ago, BioEnergen was shut down, supposedly for violating EPA standards. The facility was abandoned. I ran a search on the dark web and discovered the EPA violations were what got released to the press. In actuality, the factory was raided in a joint operation by the FBI and the CIA based on intel that they were about to sell classified information to the Russians."

Holly shook her head. "My parents were scientists, not international spies."

"No, but they were working for BioEnergen on a secret project our foreign adversaries were interested in getting their hands on."

Holly glanced across the console at Simon. "They never told me that. All they talked about was their work preserving the environment."

"I found where a Dr. Armand Duval testified that during the raid, all the data and research notes that had been compiled on the special project they'd been working on for the past two years had been erased from the company's computer database. The two scientists who'd developed the data were the masterminds behind the research and development. It was the entirety of their work that had been lost."

"Are you telling me that the two scientists were my mother and father?" Holly shook her head. "They told me they were working to save the bayou, not to work for the very kinds of corporations that threaten the existence of the bayou through negligent practices."

"Sorry, but from what I can tell, they were knee-deep in R&D for BioEnergen, an energy company looking for alternatives to oil and oil derivatives."

"It doesn't make sense," Holly said. "They were

passionate about their home, about the bayou and their work to save it. They were just as passionate about our country and wouldn't sell out to Russia."

"I went a step further and got the coordinates of the BioEnergen facility that was shut down," Swede continued. "Though it was supposed to be completely shut down, it's still drawing power. I was able to tap into satellite images generated within the past week. For a place that's supposed to be abandoned, there've been people coming and going."

"Maybe we should go there now instead of house hunting," Simon suggested.

"Since someone is targeting Holly, I thought it best to send someone else to gather intel," Swede said. "I've spoken to Remy. He's sending a two-man team out there with cameras and binoculars. They're just going out to observe, not engage."

Simon nodded. "If the people at the abandoned facility are the ones who murdered Paul, caused Holly's parents to disappear and are now using scare tactics with Holly, it might be better that they don't know we're on to them. At least until we have a little more information."

"Exactly," Swede said.

"I want to be with that two-man team," Holly said.

"You're being watched," Swede said. "To keep anyone from knowing we're observing them, you and Simon need to continue with your normal plans. That will lead your stalkers away from the team heading out into the bayou to observe and take images of the people using the facility."

Holly frowned. "I'd rather know what's going on, but I get it."

"We'll brief you as soon as the team returns with information," Swede promised. "For now, out here."

"Out here," Simon echoed and ended the call.

Holly shot a glance toward Simon, her lips twisting into a grimace. "I guess we're going to visit the seer my Mémère insisted we see about the curse and our future."

"You still think you're cursed?" Simon asked. "Curses don't cut anchoring lines or use explosive incendiary devices."

"Yeah, you're right," Holly said. "But when Mémère says to do something, you do it. She has her reasons."

Simon shrugged. "Okay. Let's go have our fortunes read by an animal."

Holly fought back a grin. She believed in Voodoo and magic. However, Simon was right. Curses didn't cut lines or set off explosives. The data Swede had accumulated about BioEnergen had made Holly lose confidence in a curse being the source of her problems.

What worried her was that she believed a curse would be easier to deal with than going toe-to-toe with murderous humans.

CHAPTER 10

THOUGH SIMON THOUGHT HAVING his fortune read was a waste of time, the drive got Holly away from Bayou Mambaloa and, hopefully, whoever was targeting her—at least for the morning.

He'd sent a text to the realtor asking to push back their appointment a couple of hours to give them time to find the seer and fulfill Madam Gautier's request.

On the drive over to the neighboring parish, Simon contacted his teammate, Beau Boyette, who'd given him the name and phone number of his cousin, Alexandra Belle, who made some calls and texted him the address and phone number of Lady LeChance.

Holly called ahead to make sure the seer was available for a consultation. Lady LaChance assured her she would be there and was expecting them.

The GPS directions took them to a gravel road on the south end of the town of Bayou Miste. The road led to a clearing and what appeared to be an oversized gypsy wagon that had been converted into a home, complete with an electric line and satellite dish.

Simon had fully expected to see a horse tied close by, but wasn't completely surprised to find a bright red, vintage Mustang convertible parked nearby. He shifted into park, dropped to the ground and met Holly at the front of the truck.

She took his hand and squeezed it. "I don't expect you to believe; just be open to suggestion."

"I'm wide open," he said, with no trace of sarcasm. "Lead the way."

They climbed the steps to the colorful gypsy wagon and knocked on the quaint, round, red door.

A petite woman dressed in a long, peasant-style skirt and top with a brightly colored scarf covering her hair opened the door. "You must be Holly," she said. "Please, come in."

When Simon stepped up behind Holly, Lady LaChance smiled up at him. "Ah, and you must be her lover, Simon."

Holly gasped.

Simon forced a smile. After all, he couldn't argue with the woman's words. The previous night, he had been Holly's lover. Whether they would ever be again...well, that remained to be seen.

"Have a seat on the cushions," she said, "while I prepare our furry fortune teller."

The cushions were large, fluffy pillows on the floor, one a deep purple, the other royal blue.

Holly sat on the purple pillow. Simon lowered himself onto the royal blue one and watched as Lady LaChance reached into a large metal cage lined with cedar shavings and removed a rodent that looked like a small beaver without the paddle-shaped tail.

She nestled the animal against her neck as she carried it over to where they sat. Lady LaChance sank onto a red cushion. In front of her stood the kind of portable tray table most people used for breakfast in bed. It had been covered with a pure white satin cloth.

"I ask that you two join hands, clear your thoughts, but for one that might be troubling you."

Having agreed to be open to the session, Simon wiped the hundred and one concerns roiling around his head and focused on keeping Holly safe. If thoughts of her lying naked next to him in the starlight intruded, he considered it all about keeping her close and safe.

"Are you focused?" the woman asked.

Holly nodded. "I am."

Lady LaChance looked past the creature in her arms and met Simon's gaze. "And you?"

"I am," Simon responded, hoping to hurry this meeting along.

"Then we shall begin." Lady LaChance held the nutria up in front of her and stared into its little, furry face.

Creature of the bayou's bend,
Whiskers twitching, truth you send
Stir the darkness, lift the veil,
Tell us what the signs entail.

She touched her nose to the creature's, closed her eyes and held that pose for a long moment.

Then the nutria pooped.

Holly squeezed Simon's hand.

Simon choked down a laugh and schooled his expression into his best poker face.

Lady LaChance opened her eyes and smiled down at the poop on the white satin cloth, studying how the pellets lay. "Well done, my dear. Well done." She held the animal out. "Take my friend," she said to Simon. "Hold him carefully while I interpret the signs."

Simon took the animal, careful to keep his fingers away from its sharp teeth. At the same time, he hung its ass over the white satin-covered tray—in case it dropped more insight on their future.

Convinced it couldn't get stranger, Simon held

the nutria and watched as Lady LaChance's eyes rolled back and her face paled. As if in a trance, she spoke slowly, her voice deep and monotone.

Love has found you, sweet and sure,
  Tho' bayou shadows prove unpure—
  Trust not those who will deceive,
  Or death'll leave a love to grieve.

The air in the wagon grew heavy. The candlelight dimmed.

Simon brought the little rodent close to his chest, the creature's warmth doing little to chase away the sudden chill surrounding them.

Holly reached over and placed her hand on the nutria, leaning her shoulder into Simon's.

Lady LaChance swayed left and right. Then she sat up straight, and her eyes snapped open.

She glanced from Holly to Simon and back. "We're done here." She folded the satin cloth with the rodent poop inside. "That will be forty dollars. You can leave it on the cushion and show yourself out." Lady LaChance stood and walked toward a door at the back of the wagon. She paused with her hand on the doorknob and glanced over her shoulder, her brow furrowed, a sad look in her eyes.

. . .

Ones you should trust will sell you cheap,
Loyalty bought, their secrets deep—
When hope runs thin, let love stay strong,
For truth will rise and right the wrong.

For a long moment, the seer stared at Simon. Then her gaze dropped to the nutria he held. "Leave Renault in the crate and secure the latch. He's quite the Houdini escape artist."

She disappeared through the door and closed it behind her.

Simon held the rodent a few moments longer, wondering what the seer had meant by all she'd said.

When Renault nipped Simon's finger, he nearly dropped the animal.

"Here, let me." Holly carried the nutria to his crate, laid him gently inside and secured the latch. Then she held out her hand.

"What?" Simon asked, his head still spinning with the seer's predictions.

"Do you have forty dollars?" Holly asked.

Simon fished his wallet from his back pocket and handed her two twenties.

Holly laid them on the red cushion, then hooked his arm and led him out of the wagon.

Once they were back in the truck, he started the engine, backed up, turned around and drove down the gravel road. He glanced one last time in the rearview mirror and shook his head. "What the hell just happened?"

"Nothing," Holly said, her gaze on the road ahead. "Just drive."

They spent the trip back to Bayou Mambaloa in silence. Several times, Simon opened his mouth to say something and closed it, shaking his head.

Usually, he didn't buy into all the supernatural bullshit, but something about the session in the gypsy wagon had set him on edge.

By the time they made it back to Bayou Mambaloa, they had to hurry to get to their meeting with LaShawnda at a home a block off Main Street.

They walked through the small bungalow painted lemon yellow with white trim. Though it was well cared for, with fresh interior paint and updated countertops, it didn't inspire more than a passing glance from Simon. Holly had little to say as well.

"I'm sorry we only have one home to view today," LaShawnda said as they left the yellow house. "The other two homeowners couldn't alter their appointment times. I'll have to set up viewings on another day."

"It's okay," Simon said. "We can do this another day." He took Holly's hand and walked with her to the truck. "Thank you for being flexible," he said to LaShawnda.

She gave him a bright smile. "I just want you to find the house that suits you most. I won't try to sell you something you don't love."

"Thank you," Holly said and climbed into the truck.

As LaShawnda drove away in her sleek black SUV, Simon sat with his hands resting on the steering wheel. "Where to?"

Holly leaned back in her seat and closed her eyes. "How about we hit the diner? We missed lunch, and I won't make it through my shift on an empty stomach."

Simon drove the few blocks to the diner, parked and rounded to the passenger side to help Holly to the ground. He pulled her into his arms for a moment and rested his cheek against her temple. "I don't know about you, but the visit with the seer sucked the life out of me."

She laughed and leaned her forehead against his chest. "I thought it was just me. I came away from Bayou Miste completely drained from our session with Lady LaChance." She leaned back and stared up at him. "Or is it we're tired from being up all night and fighting a fire this morning?"

He wrapped his arms around her and held her close. "Or are we just hungry and reading too much into her mumbo jumbo?"

"I could eat a bowl of gumbo." Holly turned and slipped her arm around his waist.

"I like the Cajun-style meatloaf," Simon said as they walked into the diner and found a booth in the far corner. They ordered their meal and ate in companionable silence, each lost in their own thoughts.

Despite his attempt to ignore what the seer had said, Simon found himself replaying her words over and over in his mind. If it was a prediction of the future, how would it play out? Who were the people he was supposed to trust, and what would they do to betray that trust?

More importantly, what love would stand strong?

He stared across the table at Holly, her auburn hair falling down around her shoulders. Beautiful, passionate and determined to learn the truth. Was she the love the seer spoke of?

Did he love Holly?

He desired her, but was that love?

She glanced up, caught him looking at her and frowned. "Do I have gumbo on my face?" she asked, dabbing her napkin over her mouth.

He smiled, loving the sparkle in her green eyes and the way her forehead wrinkled when she was thinking hard. "Maybe a little," he lied and reached out to brush his thumb across her lips. "There. Got it."

"Thanks." She set her napkin on the table. "I wish I didn't have to work tonight."

"Can't you call in sick?" Simon asked.

She shook her head. "Can't. It's all hands on deck. There's a motorcycle rally in town tonight. Rene is going to need every waitress available. He expects the Crawdad Hole to be packed. Standing room only." She sighed. "At least I'll be so busy, it will make the night pass quickly. I just feel bad for you."

"Why?"

Her lips twisted. "It can't be fun hanging out all evening in a crowded bar."

Depending on the nature of the motorcycle clubs that would be there, he might have to be especially on his toes to keep Holly safe. He shrugged nonchalantly. "I can handle it." He hoped he was right. It might be a night to ask for reinforcements from his teammates.

They finished their meals, paid the ticket, drove to the edge of town and parked behind the Crawdad Hole Bar and Grill.

Simon leaned across the console and took Holly's hand in his. "Are you going to be all right tonight?"

She pressed his palm to her cheek. "I'll be fine. Thanks for caring." Then she pressed her lips into his palm. "I'd better get inside. The parking lot is already starting to fill."

Simon followed her into the building and staked his claim on a barstool at the end of the bar, where he had his back to the wall and a good line of sight that encompassed the area Holly would work.

Within the next two hours, the place filled with

men in leather jackets, their arms, necks and any other exposed skin covered in tattoos. For the most part, the MC members were respectful of the waitresses. Not once did they try to cop a feel or grab Holly.

Still, Simon remained tense, ready to launch into action should Holly need him.

She worked the crowd, taking orders, carrying heavy trays of drinks, all the while smiling at customers.

At one point, Simon offered to carry a tray for her, but she shook her head. "I've got this."

Simon remained on his barstool, feeling guilty that he wasn't helping.

Rene slapped a plastic tub on the bar in front of Simon. "If you want to help, go collect the empties."

Simon gave the bar owner a nod. "Thanks."

Rene laughed. "Don't thank me. I'm not paying you."

With a laugh, Simon took the tub and worked his way through the tightly-packed tables, collecting the empty bottles, mugs and plates. He was sure to keep Holly in his peripheral vision, always aware of where she was and who was around her.

When Cody West pushed through the entrance, Simon frowned.

He'd prefer dealing with the motorcycle clubs over Cody any day.

Completely predictable, Cody made straight for Holly, who was carrying a heavy tray full of drinks.

Simon slammed the tub he carried on the nearest table and pushed his way through the men in leather jackets to get to Holly.

Holly, unaware of the man advancing on her, bent to unload her tray a drink at a time. She'd set the third of five in front of a customer when Cody approached her from behind.

Still too far from her to help, Simon shoved at people standing in his way.

"Hey!" A giant of a man with a shaggy gray beard hanging down over his chest, wearing a black leather jacket, stepped in front of Simon. "Calm your ass down before someone takes you out back and teaches you some manners."

Simon shook his head, his gaze on Holly talking with Cody. When the bastard grabbed for her hand, she glared at him.

"Excuse me, sir," Simon said. "My girlfriend is in trouble. I need to get to her ASAP."

The big motorcycle club member frowned and looked over his shoulder to gaze in the direction Simon had been headed. "Oh, in that case," he stepped to the side, "don't let me hold you up. Need help?"

Simon shook his head. "No, thank you. I think I can handle it for now."

"The name's Mace Lafayette," the big guy said. "Yell if you need backup."

"Thanks, Mace." Simon continued pushing his way through. When he was within three people of reaching his goal, Cody grabbed Holly and hauled her up against his barrel chest.

Simon shoved through the men in front of him, making one of them spill the beer he held.

"Son of a bitch," the man yelled.

Simon didn't stop to apologize. He reached for Cody, clamped a hand on the man's shoulder and yanked him backward and off balance.

Cody released his hold on Holly, teetered, steadied and spun, his cheeks a ruddy red, eyes blazing. "What the fuck!"

"The lady isn't into you," Simon said. "Leave her the fuck alone."

Behind Simon, a voice said, "Dude, you made me spill my beer."

He ignored the man and his beer, more intent on keeping Holly safe.

"Holly's my girl, not yours." Cody balled his fists. "And I've had about enough of your interference." As Cody cocked his arm, the man behind Simon clapped a meaty hand on Simon's shoulder. "You owe me—"

Cody swung.

Simon saw it coming and dodged to the side.

Cody's fist missed Simon and landed in the face of the biker who'd been behind Simon.

The biker roared and punched Cody.

Cody fell back into another man wearing MC leathers, who fell into another biker, and the Crawdad Hole became a free-for-all fight between biker gangs and locals.

Holly raised her tray like a shield and worked her way back to the bar.

With fists flying and men shoving, Simon couldn't fight his way through the melee to get to her fast enough.

Rene, the bar owner, rallied the wait staff and sent them to the back storeroom as he pressed his cell phone to his ear.

A man clocked Simon in the chin, spinning him around. He didn't have time to fight his way through a dozen pissed-off bikers. He had to get to Holly.

When the guy came at him again, he was ready. He dodged the punch, grabbed the man's arm as it flew past his ear, yanked it down and twisted it up and behind the guy. Then he heaved him forward, toppling the other men standing in Simon's way.

Now, with a semi-clear path, he clambered over the pileup and vaulted over the bar. As he cleared its shiny surface, the bar owner raised a small airhorn canister and blasted noise that cut through the shouts and yelling.

"Sit down and shut up or get the hell out!" Rene called out. "The sheriff's department is on the way."

A few men continued to shove, half-heartedly,

while others gathered their friends and hurried toward the door.

Simon made for the back storeroom. Before he reached the door, the waitress he knew as Danny ran out, her eyes wild. "Help! Someone help! A man grabbed Holly and carried her out the back door!"

CHAPTER 11

SIMON RUSHED PAST DANNY, blew through the storeroom and out the delivery door of the Crawdad Hole.

A truck spun gravel up as it shot out of the parking lot.

Bikers mounted their motorcycles, the engines raising a deafening roar in the night air.

Even if he could get to his truck, Simon wouldn't make it out of the parking lot with all five hundred motorcycles leaving at the same time.

"Dude," a voice called out over the roar. "Get on the back. I'll get you there."

The man who'd called himself Mace pulled up beside him on a shiny black Harley Davidson.

With no better option and the truck carrying Holly getting further away by the second, Simon slung his leg over the back seat, grabbed hold of the man's leather jacket and held on.

Mace zigzagged through the mass exodus of motorcycles. He drove down into a shallow ditch and back up to get around the slow-moving procession and back onto the road, less clogged by cyclists eager to leave before the sheriff arrived.

Mace gunned the throttle, sending the motorcycle shooting forward, passing others in a flash.

Simon leaned around the big guy, searching the road ahead until he finally spotted the taillights of the truck he hoped had Holly inside. "There!" he shouted over the roar of the engine and pointed at the truck.

Mace leaned forward, pushing the motorcycle as fast as it would go.

Without a helmet with a face shield, Simon squinted against the wind and the bugs inherent in the Louisiana night sky.

He remembered this part of the highway would come to a T intersection not much further ahead. The truck's brake lights lit up.

There.

The kidnappers had to slow down to turn right or left.

Mace zoomed forward, closing the distance between them and the truck.

The truck turned right.

Before reaching the intersection, Mace left the road, dipped down into the ditch and back up onto a gravel patch. Simon held on for dear life as they went back into a ditch and up onto the highway, arriving alongside the bed of the truck.

The driver didn't appear to notice because of the commotion in the passenger seat.

A man held Holly as she kicked and fought to free herself from his grip.

Anger burned through Simon. "Get me closer," he called out.

Mace drove to within a foot of the truck bed.

Simon braced his hands on the big guy's shoulders and pushed himself up to get his feet on the seat.

Ahead, the road curved. He had to go now or miss his chance.

Simon leaped from the back of the motorcycle into the bed of the truck, landing on his hands and knees among an array of junk and tools.

Mace dropped back behind them, keeping pace.

Once in the truck bed, Simon realized he wasn't in much better position as he'd been on the back of the motorcycle. He couldn't just step out onto the running board, yank open the door and tell the driver to stop, could he?

He peered around the side and shook his head.

Not at sixty miles per hour.

The truck's back windshield didn't have a sliding window for him to push to the side and crawl through.

The truck hit a pothole, tossing Simon to one

side. As he used his hands to right himself, his fingers wrapped around a smooth, heavy tool. He raised it to the starlight, revealing a large pipe wrench. He stood in a wide stance to better balance, swung the wrench back and then sharply forward, putting all his weight into it as he hit the back window.

Glass shattered inward, leaving a gaping, jagged hole.

The driver swerved, throwing Simon onto his backside.

Someone inside the truck muttered a long string of curses. "What the hell?"

The truck swerved back in the opposite direction.

Simon waited another moment, then crawled toward the broken window and, from a kneeling position, swung the wrench again. The remaining glass crashed inward.

"Do something. He's destroying my truck!" the driver said.

"I can't do anything..." the man holding Holly grunted, "with this..." another grunt, "bitch... Will you hold still?"

"No," Holly's voice sounded from inside the cab. "Pull over now, or my boyfriend is going to beat your scrawny asses."

"Not if I have anything to do with it," the driver said.

Simon braced himself as the driver jerked the steering wheel to the left.

"Goddamn woman," the man holding Holly shouted. "Oh, fuck, she's loose. Look out!"

Simon looked through the back window in time to see Holly lunge for the steering wheel.

She grabbed it and pulled hard.

Before the driver could correct, the truck ran off the road.

Simon dropped flat in the bed, bouncing with the junk. The truck came to an abrupt halt, flinging Simon forward. Water splashed over the sides of the bed, drenching Simon.

Simon dragged himself up to his hands and knees and looked through the broken glass.

Holly lay across the cab, trapped between the men and the dashboard, trying to untangle herself as water rushed to fill the cab.

"I can't get out of my seatbelt," the man in the passenger seat said.

"Me either, and the door won't open," the driver said. "Get her off me." He shoved at Holly.

With nowhere to go, she didn't move far.

"Have to get out," the passenger said. "Help!"

"Help!" the driver echoed.

"For Pete's sake," Holly said. "Quit bellyaching and help me get off the two of you."

"Come through the back window," Simon called out. "I'll help."

The back of the truck dipped.

Mace moved up beside Simon. "I'll help as well."

Simon found the pipe wrench and used it to sweep the last bits of broken glass from the back window. "I'm going in."

"I've got your back," Mace said and helped Simon shimmy halfway through the window.

"Holly, can you reach toward the back of the truck?"

"Only if these idiots will let go of me."

"If you let her go," Simon said, "we'll help you out as well. If you don't let go, we'll get her out without your help and leave you to drown."

"Time's running out, boys," Holly said. "What's it to be?"

"Well damn, there goes a thousand bucks," the driver said. "She's coming out." Moments later, Holly was shoved toward Simon. He grabbed her forearm and pulled her through the window, into his arms and kissed her.

She captured his cheeks between her palms and kissed him back. "I knew you'd come."

"What about us? It's getting deep in here," the passenger said.

"Much as they deserve to drown, we can't let it happen." Holly scrambled out of the way.

Before Simon could go back in, Mace handed him a wicked-looking knife like the one Simon had carried in his Delta Force days. "You might need this."

Armed with the knife, Simon pushed through the back window.

Water had risen to the point that both men trapped in their seatbelts had to tip their heads back to breathe.

Simon reached for the driver first, felt beneath the water for the seatbelt. He slid the knife under the belt and sliced through it.

By then, the water was covering the guy's face, only his nose remaining free.

Free of the belt, he pushed upward.

Simon started to move back to get out of the way, but the guy in the passenger seat captured his arm and held on with a panicked death grip. Simon fought to free his arm.

The driver attempted to push past him. In the confusion, they were all three stuck. With water rushing in, Simon had barely sucked in a breath when a hand clamped down on his ankles and yanked him backward, out of the cab, through the window and into open air.

Mace shoved him aside, reached in and pulled the driver out.

The man dropped onto the bed of the truck, coughing the water out of his lungs.

Mace pointed at the man. "Make any stupid moves and I'll shove you back in that truck and let you drown." To Simon, he said. "Go. Get the other guy."

Simon drew in a breath and dove into the truck,

felt his way to the passenger still trapped in his seatbelt, struggling to break free.

Simon sliced through the guy's belt at the same time the man managed to shove open his door. The two men swam out into the murky water and came up for air.

The man he'd just rescued turned on Simon and tried to shove him under.

Simon fought for the surface.

A shout from above made the man stop.

Simon came up to find Holly standing in the truck bed, holding the pipe wrench like a sledgehammer and looking like an avenging warrior—a wet, bedraggled warrior with flashing eyes and a fierce scowl. "That's right. You heard me. You hurt him, and I'll crush your skull and leave you for the alligators to finish off."

Simon shoved the man toward the bank. He crawled up the muddy slope and collapsed on the ground near the rear of the truck.

Mace and Holly stood nearby, with the driver seated on the ground, his wrists secured behind his back in a zip tie.

Mace jerked the other man around and cinched his wrists in another zip-tie.

Simon's lips quirked. "Your zip ties?"

Mace nodded. "Always keep a few handy. Never know when you'll need them." He shoved the man to his knees, forcing him to sit beside his cohort in crime. "Sheriff's on the way."

Simon pulled Holly close. "Are you all right?"

She nodded. "I am."

He nodded toward the guys on the ground. "Recognize these characters?"

"Sadly, I do." She shook her head. "The driver is Germain, and that's his cousin, Bubba. They're members of the Fontenot clan." Her eyes narrowed in the light from the Harley. "What the hell were you thinking?"

Germain shrugged. "Some guy offered me a thousand bucks to take you to the old cane mill. It was supposed to be an easy grand."

"Yeah. Easy." Bubba snorted. "I think she broke my rib, and I nearly drowned."

"You're lucky Holly has a soft spot for idiots," Simon said. "I would've let you drown." He stepped closer, his fists clenching at his sides. "Who paid you?"

"I don't know," Germain said. "It was a phone call from an unknown number."

Mace grabbed Germain by the front of his shirt and lifted him off the ground. "I've got a daughter about Holly's age. I'd kill any man who did that to her. It would be justice served to throw you to the alligators."

Germain's eyes rounded. "He said he wasn't going to hurt her. He wanted her alive."

Sirens wailed in the distance.

Mace held Germain a little longer, nose to nose. "You disgust me." Then he shoved him back to the ground. "I hear either one of you pull some stupid stunt like this again, I'll bring the wrath of the Bayou Reapers down on you. Got that?" He kicked dirt onto the two men.

"Got it," Bubba said. "Besides, running drugs is a helluva a lot easier than running hellcat females."

Germain kicked his cousin. "Shut up, dumbass."

Bubba glared at Germain.

Sheriff Bergeron was the first to arrive at the scene. Between him and Deputy Shelby Taylor, they loaded the two men into the back of the sheriff's SUV.

Deputy Taylor fished a dry towel out of the back of her SUV and handed it to Holly.

Holly's lips twisted in a grimace. "I thought you had the night off."

Shelby shook her head. "When the biker fight broke out at the Crawdad Hole, all deputies were called in. Fortunately, most everyone had dispersed by the time we arrived. When Rene and Danny told us you'd been taken, we weren't sure which way to go until we got the 911 call." She lifted her chin toward Mace. "Thanks."

Mace shifted on his feet. "Just want to keep the peace. We ride for pleasure and camaraderie, not to stir up trouble."

Shelby's lips spread in a smile. "I've heard of the Bayou Reapers. You've done good things to help single parents and their kids."

"We're veterans who served our country and like to give back to our community. Some of us were raised by single parents. They don't always get a break." Mace squared his shoulders. "Now, if you don't need me, I'd like to get home to my old lady before she sends my brothers out looking for me."

Simon held out his hand. "Thanks for everything."

Mace clasped his hand in a firm grip. "If you ever get a ride, we're open to new members, especially those who work for the good."

"I'd like that," Simon said.

Mace tipped his head toward Holly. "She's badass. Take care of her."

"That's my plan," Simon said.

Mace held out his hand to Holly. "Ms. Holly, we welcome female riders as well. We'd be honored for you to join us."

Holly took the man's hand and pulled him in for a hug. "Thanks for helping me."

The biker mounted his Harley and drove away.

Once Deputy Taylor had their statements, she gave them a ride back to the Crawdad Hole. "Do you need me to have a deputy positioned near your houseboat?" she asked.

"That won't be necessary," Simon said. "We'll stop by for some of Holly's things and stay the night at the boarding house." He turned to Holly. "If that's all right with you...?"

Holly nodded. "I don't have the energy to argue or to stay awake all night wondering if someone will sabotage the boat while we sleep."

Simon walked her to his truck and handed her up into the passenger seat. He stepped up onto the running board, leaned in and snapped her seatbelt in place.

"You know I can buckle my own seatbelt," she whispered into his ear.

"I know," he said, backing up just enough. "But this gives me an excuse to kiss you." He pressed his lips to hers in a gentle kiss.

Holly laced her hands behind his neck and deepened the kiss until they were both breathless. "Can we hurry by the houseboat? I'd like to get a shower and go to bed." She kissed him again. "With you."

Simon's groin tightened. "We can make that happen."

He closed her door, hurried around to the driver's side and raced out of the parking lot, eager to get to the houseboat and back to the boarding house.

All the bullshit he'd imagined, convincing himself not to get involved with her, had flown out the back of the Fontenots' truck. When he'd thought he might lose her for good, he'd realized he didn't want to be without her.

As he drove out to the houseboat, she reached across the console and took his hand in hers.

He parked in the clearing and met Holly in front of the truck. They walked hand in hand to the dock and crossed the gangway to the houseboat.

Simon slid the key into the lock and pushed open the door. "Let me go first."

Holly started to nod when a voice sounded from inside.

"That won't be necessary."

Lights flicked on, and Madam Gautier stood in the doorway, a frown creasing her forehead.

"Mémère? What are you doing here?" Holly asked. "Are you all right?"

Her grandmother shook her head. "I should be asking you the same. I hear the Fontenot boys tried to take off with you, and you all almost drowned." She reached out with a gnarled hand and cupped Holly's cheek. "This cannot continue."

Holly covered her grandmother's hand with her own. "I'm okay. I didn't drown."

Madam Gautier took her hand and stepped out onto the deck. "You must come with me." She started across the gangway.

Holly stood fast. "I'm safe with Simon."

Her grandmother looked back at them. "Both of you must come with me."

"To your house?" Holly asked. "That's not necessary. We weren't going to stay here anyway. We're going to the boarding house."

"Madam Gautier, I blame myself for what happened tonight. I didn't stay close enough to your granddaughter. I should've been at her side every minute." He reached for Holly's other hand. "But I promise I'll stick to her like glue. The boarding house has security cameras. We'll be safe there."

The older woman shook her head. "Holly won't be safe anywhere. You both need to come with me." Her face hardened. "Now. No questions asked."

When Holly opened her mouth, her grandmother held up her hand. "Trust me."

Holly glanced from her grandmother to Simon.

He felt the steel in the Voodoo queen's tone and saw the concern for her granddaughter in her eyes. "We'll come."

Holly's brow dipped briefly. Then she nodded and followed her grandmother across the gangway to the dock. Instead of turning toward land, she led them to the end of the dock where a small skiff was tied to a post. Her grandmother waited for Simon to get in first, then Holly. They held out their hands for Madam Gautier and helped her into the rocking boat.

She settled at the till, started the engine and drove the little boat out into the inky-black waters of the bayou.

After a few minutes, Holly looked back at her grandmother. "You missed the turn to your island."

Her grandmother stayed her course. "We're not going there."

"Where are we going?" Holly asked.

She glanced left then right, her brow furrowing before answering, "No questions."

Simon did a three-hundred-sixty-degree study of the land and water around them. The way Madam Gautier was acting, she suspected they were being followed.

A movement out of the corner of his eye made Simon glance toward the shadows beneath a stand of cypress trees several yards behind them. A bird burst out of the branches and flew low across the water. Nothing else moved, but that eerie feeling that someone was watching persisted.

CHAPTER 12

THE TENSION in the little skiff was so taut that Holly felt as though she would snap in half if anything jumped out at them. Her grandmother could be secretive, but something about her actions, the fact it was the middle of the night, and they were heading out into the maze of the bayou with no idea where she was taking them...

Holly sat on the bench beside Simon and slipped her hand in his. He stared forward, studying the channels in the starlight.

Holly had spent her youth on the bayou. She knew many of the channels and had navigated them day and night. Where her grandmother was taking her wasn't a place she'd been to often. She paid attention in case she had to find her way back. Hard enough in the daylight, it would be even harder at night.

Her grandmother navigated the waterways with a steady hand as if she'd taken this particular route many times. Her confidence made Holly wonder if she really knew her Mémère. So many questions bubbled up in her mind.

Her grandmother had been clear. Asking questions wouldn't be allowed or tolerated.

For thirty or more minutes, the little skiff wove through the channels, taking them deeper into the less-traveled areas.

When Holly thought they might be lost, the skiff slowed, rounded a bend and aimed straight for the weeping branches of a willow tree.

Simon and Holly parted the soft curtain as the skiff entered a shadowy grotto beneath the tree.

Holly glanced back at her grandmother, unable to make out her face in the gloom. Was this the place? This grotto deep in the bayou?

Her grandmother steered the skiff through the other side of the willow's curtain into what appeared to be a dead end. The skiff floated slowly toward a small island that rose out of the dark water. Its steep, unwelcoming banks were covered in twisted vines, discouraging anyone from setting foot on its soil.

As the skiff neared the steep banks, the island shuddered.

Holly and Simon stiffened at the same time and raised their arms in defense.

"It's okay," her grandmother said. "It won't hurt you."

The banks suddenly parted, a soft grinding noise accompanying the movement. Then, as if out of nowhere, a pale, yellow light appeared, casting a cone of light over the end of a wooden dock. The dock led away, disappearing into a strange, black abyss.

The skiff floated up beside the dock.

Simon looped a line around a piling.

The grinding, mechanical noise sounded again as the island closed around them, trapping them inside.

Holly's pulse quickened with the sudden instinct of fight or flight.

"We get out here," Mémère said softly.

"Where are we?" Holly asked.

"All will be revealed," was all her grandmother said.

Simon stepped up onto the dock and helped Holly alight beside him. Between the two of them, they handed Madam Gautier safely onto the wooden platform.

She led the way toward the utter blackness at the other end of the dock. The darkness was a solid metal wall with a metal handwheel painted the same black as the wall.

Madam Gautier waved a hand toward the wheel. "Will you do the honors?"

Simon gripped the wheel and turned it left. A

watertight bulkhead door separated from the black wall and swung open. Bright light shone out on them, revealing a hallway beyond.

Holly's grandmother stepped through the door and down a staircase.

Holly followed with Simon close behind.

The staircase led down into what could only be described as an underground bunker. Shelves full of various supplies, including canned goods, bags of dried beans, bottles of butane and other fuels, lined the tunnel they passed through. There was enough food and supplies for several people to live on for weeks, if not months.

Holly guessed the place belonged to a prepper ready for an apocalypse.

The more she studied the corridor, the more it looked like...

"This is or was a ship," Simon said. "A small one, but a ship, nonetheless." He pointed to the stenciled nomenclature on one of the walls they passed. "I'd bet it's either a decommissioned Navy vessel or an old Army ship.

"It's a decommissioned 1955 Coast Guard Cutter," a deep voice came to them from ahead of them in the corridor. "It's been converted into a self-contained bunker with its own power source and satellite connections to allow connection to the outside world without being detected." A man wearing Bermuda shorts and a black T-shirt padded barefoot toward them. His salt and pepper hair was buzzed to within less than an inch long on his head, though his face sported at least a day or two's worth of gray beard. He held out his hand to Simon. "Joe Middleton," he said. "You must be Sinclaire Sevier, former Delta Force, now working with Remy Montagne's Brotherhood Protectors."

Simon took the man's hand, although hesitantly. "You have the advantage."

"Madam Gautier has been keeping us informed of everything happening in Bayou Mambaloa, including the return of her granddaughter after a year spent in Atlanta." Joe held out his hand to Holly. "Holly, it's nice to finally meet you. I've heard so much about you."

Holly shook her head. "I'm sorry, I've heard nothing about you." She waved her hand around. "What is this place, and why are we here? And who else is here besides you?"

"Actually, this is my home. I've been working on it since I left the Marine Corps twenty years ago. I'd had my fill of being around a lot of people after twenty-five years on active duty. I spent some of my savings on an old boat I'd planned to strip and sell for salvage, but fell in love with her and made her my home." His face grew serious. "As for who else is here..." He met Holly's grandmother's gaze for a moment.

When she gave him an almost imperceptible

shake of her head, he nodded, his lips pressing into a tight line.

"Well..." he continued. "You'll see. Follow me." Joe turned and led the way deeper into the ship, passing closed doors until he came to what might once have been the dining hall.

On one side of the dining hall, the tables were crowded with the kind of equipment used in a biological lab like the one Holly's parents had worked in for years, with centrifuges, microscopes, PH meters, Bunsen burners, dry ovens and so much more.

"We didn't have a separate room we could turn into a laboratory, so we erected a wall down the middle of the dining hall and filled one side with what we needed for the lab, but still had use of the other side for meals."

"What are you studying here?" Holly asked.

Joe waved a hand toward the dining room. "I'll let the other members of the team brief you on that." He stepped back, allowing them to enter the dining hall, where a man and a woman wearing lab coats rose from a table.

The blood rushed from Holly's head. She swayed and reached for Simon.

His arm came up around her and pulled her close, or she would have fallen.

"Mom? Dad?" Tears welled in Holly's eyes, blurring her vision.

"Holly," they both said as one and hurried forward.

Arms wrapped around her, pulling her into embraces she'd thought she would never experience again.

"What?" Holly sobbed. "Why? I thought you were dead."

"Oh, honey." Evangeline Gautier brushed the hair back from Holly's forehead. "I'm so sorry. We couldn't contact you. We had to be dead on all accounts to continue our work."

Holly stood back, frowning. Her gut knotted tightly. "You let me believe you and Dad were dead."

Her mother nodded. "After they shut down the facility, Paul was killed as a warning. We knew our work was jeopardized, and you were at risk. We thought it best if everyone believed we were dead.

"We staged our 'death' with a little help from an old friend," her father tipped his head toward Joe, "and Maman." He reached out and hugged his mother, Holly's Mémère.

Holly backed away from the four of them, her gaze landing on her grandmother, who'd been complicit in the lie. "And you knew all this time?"

The Voodoo queen met her gaze and held it. "The less you knew and the more you believed they were dead, the more likely everyone else would believe it, too."

Her mother reached out to capture her hands.

"We knew you would find a way to support yourself and guessed you might leave the state to keep yourself safe."

"Did you ever think that I might miss you?" Holly pressed a hand to her chest, a sob rising up her throat. "That your deaths would break my heart?" Tears spilled down her cheeks.

Simon moved closer, his hand resting at the small of her back. He didn't try to pull her into his arms, but he was there for her.

Unlike her parents.

And her grandmother had been in on it all this time.

Holly's eyes narrowed. "When I came to you about the possibility that I was cursed, you were the one who suggested I move away from Bayou Mambaloa. The apartment in Atlanta was your idea. A friend of yours, my fanny!"

Her grandmother nodded. "It worked, didn't it?"

"And changing my name from Gautier to Hazard?"

Her Mémère shook her head. "That was all on you, but another stroke of genius."

"It didn't keep them from finding you," her father said, "but it gave us time to continue our work and kept them from moving forward."

Her mother exchanged a glance with her father. "We have to tell her everything."

"Damn right, you do." Holly crossed her arms over her chest, anger overshadowing the joy of seeing her parents alive. She'd get to the joy again, but the level of betrayal hurt.

"Come, take a seat," her mother said. "We just made a pot of coffee, and we have fresh-baked cookies Joe made."

Holly didn't want to sit. Didn't want to have coffee and cookies like any other day.

Her parents were alive!

And they'd lied to her for the last six months.

And her grandmother had lied.

"You really don't think much of me," Holly said as she sank into a chair. "I'm true to family. I could've kept your secret. You could've trusted me. Instead, you let me grieve this whole time."

"Oh, sweetie," her mother reached for her hand. "We never wanted to hurt you. It nearly broke our hearts to cut ourselves off from you."

"But it was for your safety," her father said. "There's a lot involved here. We had to play dead to keep them from taking all of our work."

Holly raised her hands to her face, suddenly so tired she ached. "Them? Who is 'them'? And how is it that you led me to believe you worked for Bayou Resilience when you were working for BioEnergen all along? You've been lying to me for years."

Her mother drew in a deep breath and let it out

slowly. "We did start out working for Bayou Resilience. You know how much we love everything about the bayou. We also know big corporations can decimate the ecosystem by dumping toxic chemicals into the water, and that the continued reliance on fossil fuels will bring drilling for oil closer and closer."

Her father leaned his elbows on the table. "We wanted to do more to help the bayou and the world.

"Coming up with an eco-friendly, renewable source of energy would save the world from the overuse of coal and oil, the dangers of spills and the destruction of habitat offshore drilling can create.

"People have tried to find alternatives to fossil fuels. No one has been able to create something sustainable."

"We have," her mother said softly. She smiled and reached over to take her husband's hand. "We were so close six months ago, but discovered our research was being leaked to the Russians. They wanted to weaponize the formula we were trying to create to replace fossil fuels."

"We were so buried in our work, we didn't realize any of that was happening until the FBI and CIA raided the facility. Your mother and I had a protocol in place that if anyone attempted to get into our online encrypted files, the data would be erased from the main computers."

Holly's mother's lips twisted. "When the raid occurred, the erasure happened as planned."

Her father cleared his throat. "The feds interrogated us and wanted to take us into custody, even though we hadn't been the ones to sell out to the Russians. Since all the data had disappeared, they couldn't prove we were building an energy source or that we were selling it to the Russians. They had to let us go. Their raid was a bust, so they cooked up an EPA violation and shut down the entire factory."

"Later that night, when we got back home, we found that our house had been ransacked, and the safe containing our backup laptop was gone. Laptop and all," her mother said, staring down at her hands curled round her coffee mug. "They had taken the research data. All of it."

Her father's lip curled up on one side. "I never felt comfortable storing the information at the house for just the possibility of what ended up happening. To ensure unauthorized persons couldn't access all the information, I set up the most critical files, containing key formula data, with additional security measures, including retinal scans. Your mother's and mine. If someone tried to hack into the file more than three times, like the main computer, the data would be erased."

Evangeline Gautier gave a tight smile. "Whoever took the safe and the laptop would only get so far with the formula and then be stopped when they tried to open the encrypted file."

"Which was all well and good until they came looking for us." Holly's father's mouth formed a tight line. "The message on the cypress tree and Paul's murder were warnings to us to give them the secrets in that file. The day we found the message in the sand near our house, we knew we had to destroy their ability to use you to get to us..."

"...to get to the data." Her mother reached for her father's hand. "Because we were the only ones who could get into that file, we had to die so they'd think they couldn't open that file. They could access enough of the formula to get a good start on what we were working on, but it would take them another two years to refine it. Even then, we weren't done. It was still unstable. Since we went into hiding, we've completed the formula and added secret safeguards to keep anyone from weaponizing it."

"How did you continue your research if they took your laptop?" Holly asked.

Her mother's lips curled in a smile. "Your father, ever the pessimist—"

"I prefer the term realist," he said.

"Ever the realist," her mother corrected, "your father had a backup to the backup stored in our boat."

"I contacted my old friend Joe," Holly's father said. "Or rather, my mother contacted him because he'd gone off grid a number of years ago. Maman knew where to find him because he'd found her when he'd been terribly sick, and she'd taken him back to his place to nurse him back to health."

Joe dipped his head toward Madam Gautier. "I owe her my life."

Madam Gautier waved a hand. "You owe me nothing. I owe you my son's and daughter-in-law's deaths." She gave a brief smile at the irony. "They would not be alive today had you not helped them stage their deaths."

"How did you flip the boat?" Holy asked her father.

"I didn't." He nodded toward Joe. "He did."

All gazes turned to Joe.

Joe shifted in his seat. "That was the fun part, although it went against the grain to sink such a beautiful boat."

Holly's father sighed. "It had to be done to keep my wife and daughter safe. With us dead, they had no reason to go after Holly."

"Until they did." Holly's eyes narrowed.

"So your grandmother said." Evangeline's lips pressed together. "All we can figure is that whoever has been working on the formula is frustrated. And since our bodies never turned up, they might've brought you back to Bayou Mambaloa in case we aren't dead."

"They're threatening you," Simon said, "to flush out your folks."

"You have the formula now, so why are you still in hiding?" Holly asked.

"We don't know who to trust." Her mother tapped her fingernail on the table. "Someone at BioEnergen knew about the protocol to destroy the data and knew we had a backup. We think whoever he is works for someone else, higher up the food chain. Someone in the US government who knew about our work. Someone who could mobilize the FBI and CIA to storm the facility, which would destroy the files stored on the database and provide enough of a distraction they could get the backup from our house before anyone would find out."

Her mother shook her head. "He didn't know the data would be rendered incomplete when they couldn't access the file. They've probably had someone working to fill the gaps, but not getting anywhere. And whoever sold the data to the Russians is getting pressured to deliver."

"Bottom line is, we don't yet know how high up the betrayal goes," Bastian Gautier said. "And you're not safe. Not when they can use you as leverage to get to us. Joe says you can stay here, and we're hoping we can hire Simon's team of Brotherhood Protectors to ferret out the players."

Simon nodded. "I think they'd be willing to provide support for the mission."

Holly pressed her lips together. "Though it's kind of Joe to offer to harbor me in his home, I'm not going to be frightened into hiding. These scare tactics have to stop."

Her mother's brow furrowed. "But you've already been targeted. They might get more aggressive." She sighed. "The other alternative is to surrender ourselves to them if they'll promise to leave you alone."

CHAPTER 13

EVEN BEFORE HER mother finished her sentence, Holly was shaking her head. "This is a case that threatens national security. You can't turn yourselves over to the bad guys. They'll use your knowledge to build weapons they can use against our country." She reached for her mother's hands. "Promise me you won't do it. Promise."

Her mother stared into her eyes, her frown deepening. "I'm sorry our work got Paul killed and put you and our country in danger. Had I known this would be the result, we would've stuck to lobbying the state to protect the bayou."

"We can't change the past," Simon said.

"No, we can't," Evangeline said. "Otherwise, we would never have teamed with BioEnergen."

Simon's eyes narrowed. "Something our data guru learned in researching your disappearance is that though the BioEnergen facility was shut down, it's still drawing electricity."

Bastian and Evangeline Gautier directed their attention to Simon.

"It's supposed to be completely shut down," Bastian said. "Abandoned,"

"We sent a recon team out to observe and report back." Simon dug in his pocket where he'd deposited his rabbit's foot and cell phone after their shower earlier. He pulled out his cell phone, hoping the earlier dunking in the water hadn't affected its functionality. Sadly, the screen was gray—no digital clock or temperature displayed in bright colors. No amount of turning it on achieved that result. He turned to Holly.

She shook her head. "Mine was just as waterlogged. I left it at the houseboat."

Simon glanced at Joe. "I don't suppose you can get a call out?"

The former Marine's lips pulled upward in a smile. "I might live off-grid, but I have access to satellites, which gives me internet and cell phone service." He held up one of the newer smartphone models. "Who do you want to call?"

"Since you have internet, we might want to do a video call."

"Can do." Joe spun toward the lab side of the dining room. "Follow me."

They all rose from the table and entered the lab.

On the far side of the room, an array of monitors was mounted on the wall, with a keyboard on the desk below.

Joe hurried across and touched a key. The monitors blinked to life, displaying various angles outside the bunker, lit only by starlight.

He hit another key that brought up another screen with a place to enter a phone number. "Who do you want to call?"

"I'd like to do a three-way with Remy Montagne and our computer guy, Swede. We can start with Remy."

Joe stepped back. "You know the numbers; you enter them."

"Mr. and Mrs. Gautier and Madam Gautier, you might want to step away from the camera." Simon waved them away from the monitors and the camera mounted above. "Like you said, the fewer people who know you're alive, the better. You, too, Joe."

Joe moved to the side with the Gautiers.

Thankfully, Simon remembered Remy's number, keyed it in and initiated the video call.

Remy answered immediately from what appeared to be the conference room inside the boat factory. "Simon, I'm glad you called. We've been trying to get in touch with you for the past hour. Shelby told us what happened at the Crawdad Hole and the attempt to kidnap Holly. Then you disappeared. Shelby even drove by the boathouse and said no one was home."

Simon held up his dead cell phone. "My cell phone went with me into the water and no longer works."

"Where are you?" Remy asked.

"I'd rather not say at this moment. I'll fill you in when we're face-to-face."

His brow creasing, Remy nodded. "Okay."

"I was hoping your recon team has news on the BioEnergen facility."

"That's why I was trying to contact you," Remy said. "Hold one and let me bring Swede online." Moments later, the screen divided into two displays, one with Remy, the other with Swede.

Swede came up with a concerned frown denting his forehead. "Simon, I heard you and Holly ran into some trouble earlier."

"We did, but we're okay for now." He reached for Holly's hand and brought her into range of the camera. "What did they find out about the BioEnergen facility?"

"Let me bring up some of the video they sent." Swede disappeared, and a grainy video of a building appeared on the screen. No lights shone on the corners or over exterior doors.

"As the satellite images indicated, there are people at this site," Swede said. "If you'll look closely, you'll see armed guards standing in the shadows at the corners and doors. At one point, the guards escorted two people into the building. Watch."

In the video, the shadowy figures of four guards appeared to approach a side entrance with two unarmed men in between. When the door opened, light shone on the faces of the men flanked by the guards.

"They were able to zoom in..."

The images grew larger, trained on the faces of the two men, getting a clear picture of each.

A gasp sounded from the direction of the Gautiers.

Simon tapped the mute button. "We're on mute," he said.

"The gray-haired man is Dr. Harlan Jeffries, our old boss," Mrs. Gautier said. "He worked with us as an employee of BioEnergen."

Mr. Gautier added, "Though he's a scientist, he wasn't in the weeds of our project. His role was more of management, expediting logistics, making sure we had the resources we needed."

Simon unmuted the mic. "The man with the gray hair is Dr. Harlan Jeffries, a former employee of BioEnergen."

"Correct," Swede said. "We were able to find his employee record and photo. The other guy in the photo is more interesting. He didn't show up in the employee database, so we ran facial recognition software on him. My counterpart, Kyla Russell, thought he looked familiar, and she was right."

Another image appeared on the screen, showing

men in suits at what appeared to be a lavish party, with women dressed in cocktail dresses and expensive jewelry. The man with Dr. Jeffries in the previous picture stood at the elbow of another man Simon recognized. "Isn't that Marcus Solberg, the billionaire tech giant?"

"That's him. The man at his elbow is his trusted fixer, Gunnar Reznik."

"Fixer?" Holly asked.

"Bodyguard, bouncer, enforcer," Swede said. "What Solberg needs done, he executes. Though some think he's been responsible for the disappearances of several of Solberg's corporate spies, no one could get enough evidence to convict him."

"What's he doing with BioEnergen?" Simon asked.

"We did some digging into the ownership of BioEnergen. Its corporate stock tanked when the feds shut it down. Several companies swooped in and bought the stock at bargain basement prices. One of those companies was a subsidiary of one of Solberg's holding companies. Another company that bought a significant number of shares belongs to a private foundation linked to—get this— the U.S. Secretary of State, Edmund Carver."

Simon glanced toward Bastian and Evangeline Gautier.

Evangeline pressed her hand to her mouth, her eyes widening.

Swede continued. "The Secretary of State recently

performed a diplomatic mission to meet with Russia's Ministry of Energy."

"BioEnergen was working on an energy alternative to fossil fuels," Holly said.

"Which tracks with everything we know about the company and its new owners. Some insider trading is going on there. Also note in the photo of Solberg and Reznik. The woman on the other side of Solberg is Lisa Carver, and beside her is her husband, Edmund Carver. The party was thrown by Solberg. He invited numerous CEOs of tech companies, a dozen billionaires, US and foreign, and US politicians to whose campaigns he contributed significant sums of money."

"Major conflicts of interest all around," Holly murmured.

"Do we have an address where Dr. Jefferies lives?" Simon asked. "Think we could get him alone long enough to question him?"

"I've got an address in Thibodaux where he lives with his wife, Amy Jefferies," Swede said. An address appeared on the screen.

Holly grabbed a pen and paper and jotted it down.

"Remy? Still with us?" Simon asked.

The photo images disappeared, replaced by Remy's and Swede's faces.

"I'm here," Remy said.

"We don't have any evidence that something illegal is going on in the BioEnergen facility, but..."

Remy nodded. "I'll talk with Shelby and Sheriff Bergeron. They might want to investigate activity in a supposedly closed facility."

"You might hold off sending anyone until Holly and I've had a chance to pay a visit to the Jeffries' home in Thibodaux," Simon said.

"Will do, but I think I'll put the rest of the team on standby in case you need back up to keep Ms. Gautier safe."

"Thanks." Simon cocked an eyebrow. "Anything else?"

Swede chuckled. "Wasn't that enough?"

"More than enough," Holly said.

"You two be careful out there," Remy said. "Seems like things could be heating up. Do you want me to send a different member of the team to talk with the Jeffries?"

"No." Holly shook her head. "Dr. Jefferies knew my folks. He might be more open to me than a stranger."

"Anything we can do in the meantime?" Remy asked.

"No. Swede—" Simon started.

"I'll keep digging into the Carver-Solberg connection to see if we can find any legally nefarious dirt on the two. If that's all, then, out here."

"Out here," Remy echoed.

The faces disappeared, leaving Simon and Holly staring at a blank screen.

"Wow," Holly turned to Simon. "That's a lot to process."

"Dr. Jeffries didn't look happy in those pictures," Evangeline said.

"He was surrounded by four guards and Solberg's bouncer." Bastian's brow dipped. "Think he's there on his own steam?"

"If they're trying to recreate the formula, they might have enlisted him to do it."

"Does he know enough to succeed?" Simon asked.

Both Evangeline and Bastian shook their heads.

"He hasn't been hands-on in years," Bastian said, "and he wasn't fully engaged in the specifics of the formula."

Holly's brow furrowed. "Which could be why they're now hoping to flush you two out since no bodies were found with the flipped boat."

"So, what's next?" Joe asked.

"Should we come out of hiding?" Evangeline asked.

"No," Holly and Simon said as one.

Holly shook her head. "They've been playing me to get to you...in case you were still alive. Let's keep them in the dark and let us see if we can get to Dr. Jeffries."

"Isn't it too dangerous to talk to Jeffries?" Bastian asked. "That fixer, Reznik, might take the opportunity to grab Holly."

"I need to do this," Holly said. "We'll be extra

careful and check things out before we try to make contact."

Madam Gautier, who'd been silent for much of the discussion, said, "I don't have a good feeling about this."

"Madam, you should stay here with Bastian and Evangeline," Simon said. "Joe will keep you safe."

"And who will keep you safe?" the Voodoo queen asked.

Simon let out a deep breath. "We'll be careful and ask for help if we need it from my team. And we'll get back up from the sheriff's department if things blow out of proportion."

Madam Gautier approached Simon. She reached around her neck and untied a leather strap with a small red velvet bag attached. "You must take this gris-gris bag. It will protect you and bring you luck."

Simon took the gift. "I don't need luck," he said. "Holly should wear this." He held the gris-gris bag out to Holly.

She shook her head. "She gave it to you."

"But I already have a lucky charm." He pulled the rabbit's foot out of his pocket. "A very good friend gave it to me. I've kept it with me since." He didn't tell them that the lucky rabbit's foot hadn't proved lucky for his friend. They didn't need to know that. And he didn't believe a gris-gris back or a lucky rabbit's foot really provided any luck.

Madam Gautier stared at him for a long moment,

her eyes narrowed. "You aren't ready to believe." She nodded to Holly. "Wear it. It will keep you safe."

"Yes, Mémère." Holly turned around so that Simon could tie the necklace around her neck. When he was finished, he leaned close and whispered, "Think you can get us back to the houseboat without your grandmother's help?"

She smiled up at him. "Yes."

He straightened and said, "We'll get going. I'd like to check out the Jeffries' place at night, though we'll likely not try to make contact until daylight. I don't want to risk being shot for intruding in the middle of the night."

"You won't be staying at the houseboat, will you?" Madam Gautier asked.

"No, we'll sleep at the boarding house," Holly said. She hugged her mother and father. "I'm still angry that you let me believe you were dead, but I'm happy that you aren't. I love you both so much."

"And we love you, too." Her mother kissed her cheek.

"Love you, baby girl," her father said and kissed her forehead. "I hope we can put this all behind us soon and live a normal life." He slipped an arm around his wife's waist.

Joe walked them through the corridor and out onto the dock. "I'll keep them safe."

"Keep them here, even if you have to sit on them," Holly said.

Simon shook Joe's hand. "Thank you."

Simon stepped into the boat and held out a hand to help Holly in. Simon sat on the bench in the middle.

Holly took the seat at the rear, pulled the cord to start the little engine and waited while the fake island hill parted, and starlight shone down on the dark water.

She drove the little boat into the weeping willow branches and out the other side.

"Did that just happen?" Holly said softly, though loud enough to be heard over the engine.

Simon glanced back. "Your parents are alive."

She nodded, starlight reflecting off the tears in her eyes. "How can I be so happy and so mad at the same time?" She gave a laugh that sounded more like a sob.

"Be happy, Holly. They were only trying to protect you."

"Yeah. I get that. I just hate that I spent so many months grieving when I could've helped."

"Can't change the past. But we can help them now."

She nodded and focused on the channels ahead.

Simon's head was on a swivel, maintaining a three-hundred-sixty-degree vigil. The revelations exposed in Joe's bunker were staggering. The people involved, if caught, had a lot to lose, financially and politically. If Holly or her parents were caught, they had even more to lose. They could lose their lives.

Simon was beginning to think he needed to ask Remy for that backup. He'd do that as soon as he got back to shore. They'd go straight to the boat factory and hope Remy was still there. If not, they'd go to Remy's house.

He needed to get another cell phone ASAP. How the hell could he request backup without a way to make that call?"

They made it back to the dock where the houseboat was moored, shrouded in darkness. They should have left a light on.

But no matter, they weren't staying.

Holly cut the engine and let the skiff float the rest of the way. After listening to the motor's constant hum, the silence seemed almost deafening. Not even the cicadas and frogs dared break the quiet.

Simon secured the line to a piling on the dock and stepped out of the boat. He reached down and gripped Holly's hand, helping her up onto the dock and into his embrace.

She wrapped her arms around him and rested her forehead against his chest. "I'm scared."

He tightened his hold.

"Not for me," she said. "But for them."

"I'm worried as well." He lifted her chin and brushed his lips across hers. "I just need one thing from inside the houseboat, then we can head out. Do you need anything?"

"My toothbrush," she said.

"We have extras at the boarding house. I just want to grab my bag." Simon led the way across the gangway, intent on getting inside and grabbing his handgun out of his go-bag. He hadn't carried it up to that point but was convinced he should. The people they were dealing with were greedy and ruthless.

He'd feel better if he was armed.

He slipped the key into the lock and pushed the door open.

A light blinked on.

Simon froze. A man stood in front of him holding a gun in his hand. With his hand still on the door, Simon jerked it closed and yelled, "Holly, run!"

"Too late," a voice said behind him.

He turned to find Solberg's fixer with his hand hanging onto Holly's hair, a gun pressed to her temple. "Make any stupid moves, and I'll blow her head off."

CHAPTER 14

THE HAND in her hair pulled so hard, Holly's eyes watered.

The man had sneaked up so silently she hadn't heard him. She hadn't known he was there until he'd grabbed a handful of her hair and yanked her head back.

She hadn't even had time to scream before he'd pressed the cold, hard barrel of a gun to her temple.

As Simon yelled, "Holly, run!" he'd spun toward her.

The guy holding her hair said, "Make any stupid moves, and I'll blow her head off."

Simon stood still and slowly raised his hand. "Don't hurt her."

"I won't as long as you do exactly as I say." The man pulled on her hair, making her lean back to ease the pain.

"Down on your knees," he demanded, "and hands behind your head."

Simon dropped to his knees and clasped his hands behind his head.

The guy behind him stuck his handgun in his waistband and grabbed Simon's wrists, securing them with a zip tie.

"Get his ankles," Holly's captor said.

The man following orders kicked Simon's feet together behind him and secured his ankles with another long zip tie.

Movement in the water past the end of the houseboat caught Holly's eye.

A pirogue floated silently in the shadow of the houseboat, captained by Holly's cousin Lissette.

She stared at Holly, her eyes round and wary.

When she started toward the dock, Holly gave a small shake of her head and mouthed the word, "No."

Lissette pushed back into the shadows and waited.

Once the man had secured Simon's ankles, he shoved Simon hard.

With his hands and his ankles bound behind him, Simon had no way to balance. He fell onto his side.

"Leave him alone!" Holly cried.

"Oh, we will," the guy holding her hair said, his tone low and dangerous. "We'll leave him alone...in the water."

"No!" Holly lurched forward, the hand in her hair keeping her from getting any closer to Simon.

The guy who'd secured his wrists and ankles grabbed under Simon's arms and dragged him to the edge of the dock.

"Don't do it," Holly said. "I'll do anything. Just don't do this." Tears welled in her eyes. "Please, don't hurt him."

"Come on, bitch." The man holding her hair in his fist pulled her toward the other side of the dock, where a boat was tied to a piling.

Holly glanced back. "No! Simon!"

The other man tried to roll Simon into the water.

Simon drew his legs in and jettisoned them out, catching the man in the chest and sending him over the edge of the dock. A loud splash sounded.

Moments later, the guy came up cursing. "Son of a bitch." He climbed up a nearby ladder, stomped over to where Simon struggled, but he finally managed to sit up.

His tormentor waited until Simon was upright, then he plowed into him, shoving as hard as he could, pushing him over the edge.

"No!" Holly cried out. "He'll die!"

The man who'd pushed him in turned with a malevolent smile. "That's the idea." He pulled another zip tie out of his wet back pocket and advanced on Holly. He yanked her arms behind her back and slapped the zip tie on her wrists.

His boss shoved his weapon into the waistband of his jeans and then stepped into the boat.

At that moment, Holly could see the man who'd held her at gunpoint. "Gunnar Resznik."

"And you're Holly Gautier. Get in the boat."

She lifted her chin but didn't move. "Why?"

"Because you're coming with us," Gunnar said.

"No."

The man behind her grabbed her around the middle and dropped her into the boat. She fell forward, landing on her knees, almost face-planting against a bench.

After the second man got into the boat, Gunnar started the engine, spun it around and blasted out into the bayou.

Holly struggled to see over the side of the boat where Simon had gone into the water. His wrists had been bound behind his back and his ankles cinched together. He wouldn't have much time to figure out how to get to the surface.

Holly's heart ached. She maneuvered to her knees and tried to throw herself overboard.

Gunnar yelled to the other guy. "Hold her or she'll get away."

Big, meaty arms wrapped around, holding her back from the edge as they got further and further away from the dock with the houseboat and Simon, lying at the bottom of the bayou.

"Why are you doing this?" she demanded.

"We need your parents," Gunnar said. "You're the bait."

"They died in a boating accident."

"Wrong," he smirked. "Try again. When they learn we have their daughter, they'll suddenly come back to life."

"But you don't understand. They're dead," she said. "They're not coming back to life."

"If they don't come for you, we'll have no reason to keep you. At that point, you can join your boyfriend."

Her dead boyfriend, lying at the bottom of the bayou.

"No, please, no," she prayed. *Please be okay. Please. Lissette, please help Simon.*

AS SOON AS Simon hit the water, he fought to turn himself upright so that his feet hit bottom first. If he could do that, he might be able to bounce to the surface for air. Failure wasn't an option. They had Holly. He had to get out of the water and go after her.

As much as he twisted and turned, he couldn't get his feet to hit bottom first. He went all the way down on his side, sinking into the silt. There, he bunched his legs and tried to get them beneath him. Already, his lungs burned for air. If he stayed down much longer...

The more he tried, the more silt he stirred.

His chest hurt with the need to breathe. Much longer and he'd suck water in, instead of air.

Something bumped against him. His first thought was that it was an alligator. When a hand grabbed his arm, he realized it was a human. That human was holding onto him at the same time as they kicked, sending them upward.

When his head cleared the surface, he sucked in a breath and then sank beneath the surface. God, he felt helpless. Again, the hand dragged him up.

"Hold on," a breathless, female voice called out. "I've got you."

Then her hand slipped, and he went under again.

This time, she grabbed hold of his hair and dragged him upward.

He did his best to kick his bound legs to keep coming up for air.

"Holly?"

"No. Lissette," she said. "They took Holly. I have a knife, but I can't hold onto the ladder at the same time as I saw at the zip ties. We'll go under for a moment."

"Just do it."

With one hand, she felt her way around to the zip tie at his back. "Okay. Deep breath."

Simon drew in a breath.

Lissette let go of the ladder on the pier. They sank together, her hands working to place the knife between his wrists. Once there, she sawed at the plastic as they continued to descend, all the way to the bottom, where their feet sank into the silt.

Then the knife broke through the plastic zip tie, and his hands were free.

Simon pushed off the bottom, kicked his bound feet and pushed at the water with his hands until he broke the surface, filling his lungs with precious air.

Lissette came up beside him, gasping.

He guided her to the ladder on the dock and grasped the rungs. For a moment, he breathed in and out. Finally, he asked. "Do you still have the knife?"

She held out a slim, bejeweled knife. "A girl can never have too many accessories," she said and climbed up the ladder.

With the knife, Simon bent and sliced through the zip tie around his ankles, then climbed up to the dock. "Did they say where they were taking her?"

Lissette shook her head. "No."

"Do you have a cell phone?"

"In my pirogue," she said. "I'll get it." She went over the side of the dock, dropping down into the small boat tied to the piling. She found the phone and handed it up to him before climbing back onto the deck.

Simon called Remy.

"Simon, you made it back?"

"We were ambushed," Simon said. "They took Holly. I figure they'll call the office of the Brotherhood Protectors to make their demands."

"I have Shelby with me at the boat factory. Got an incoming call as we speak with no caller ID." Remy said. "Putting you on hold."

Simon put the phone on speaker and paced as he waited for Remy to come back.

"What's going on?" Lissette came to stand beside him.

"Hopefully, Remy's getting the call from Holly's kidnappers to give their demands."

"Let's get into some dry clothes." Simon placed the phone on speaker and hurried into the houseboat. "Holly's clothes are upstairs."

Lissette ran up the steps.

Simon shucked his jeans and pulled on his last clean pair from his go-bag. Then he yanked his wet T-shirt over his head and dragged a dry one on, the fabric sticking to his still damp body.

Lissette descended the stairs wearing loose-fitting jeans and a faded T-shirt. She carried a pair of sneakers. "Everything's a little big on me, but still better than wet."

Simon was tying his spare running shoes when Remy came back. "They want Holly's parents to come to the BioEnergen facility in one hour—by themselves, or they'll kill Holly. If they bring the cops, they'll kill her. If they bring our Brotherhood Protectors..."

"They'll kill her," Simon said. "I get the picture. So, what's the plan?"

"We get the sheriff involved, bring our entire team and get Holly back."

"You said they'll kill her if her parents don't show up alone. You can't go in guns blazing. Her parents have to show up."

"We can't let them have Holly's parents. If the Russians get the formula, they'll weaponize the energy and use it against our country and others. They're already causing enough problems without adding additional weapons to their arsenal."

"To save Holly, we have to send in her parents," Simon insisted. And he had to figure out how to navigate the bayou even with the GPS location.

Lissette placed a hand on his arm. "They're expecting a man and a woman. It'll be dark. They won't know they have the wrong couple at first. Maybe we'll have long enough to make the trade for Holly and get all the backup we need in place."

Simon stared at Lissette, her proposal blossoming in his head. "I can go in for Mr. Gautier."

"And for *Mrs*. Gautier?" Remy asked. "Shelby wants to go in her place."

"Shelby's blond," Lissette pointed out. "Holly's mom has darker hair. You need someone with dark hair. I'll go in as Evangeline."

"It's too dangerous," Simon said.

"I don't care," Lissette said. "If it gets us inside and Holly out, that's what matters. I want to do this. Let me help my cousin." She held Simon's gaze in the starlight. "You can trust me to do this. I promise, I might not always say or do the right thing, but I love my cousin and my aunt and uncle."

"We don't have much time," Remy said.

"If you come with me, you have to follow my instructions," Simon said.

Lissette nodded. "I will. I promise. Now, we'll need disguises. Can we get lab coats? We need to look like scholarly scientists."

"I'll see what I can do," Remy promised.

Lissette ducked into the bathroom and emerged with a brush, going to work on the tangle of her long, wet hair. She pulled it back into a severe, tight knot at the nape of her neck. With her face free of makeup, the difference in the clothes and hairstyle changed her appearance from the usual sultry seductress to a serious scientist.

Simon began to believe they might get away with the charade.

"The fastest way to get to the facility is by water," Remy said. "Do you have a boat?"

"We do," Simon said.

"It should take approximately twenty minutes by water to get to the facility. I'll text the GPS pin for the location to the number you're calling from."

A text pinged through. Simone checked the pin on the map application. "Got it."

Simon could hear the tapping of a keyboard in Remy's background. "Shelby just left. She's swinging by the coroner's office for white lab coats. She'll be there in less than ten minutes."

Simon wanted to say hurry, but they needed to have everything and everyone in place before they attempted to make the trade of scientists for Holly.

"I put out an SOS call to all Bayou Brotherhood Protectors," Remy said. "So far, seven out of our ten have responded. I expect to have everyone here within fifteen minutes. Shelby is mobilizing the sheriff's department on the down-low in case the people at BioEnergen are listening to the police scanner. Sheriff Bergeron is fueling up the sheriff's department's watercraft."

"How do you plan to get the team out to BioEnergen's location?" Simon asked.

"Working on that," Remy said. "Just woke Mitchell Marceau. He's headed to the marina to prep rentals. Should have them ready when our guys get there. Our newest recruit, Anton Noel, a former Air Force PJ, just let me know he's bringing a drone so we can get eyes in the sky."

"Now, all we need is the National Guard, SEAL Team 6 and the Bayou Reapers," Simon said. "Seriously, I'm worried they'll have sentries positioned around the complex and will spot the army of people converging before Lissette and I can get inside."

"And I'm not excited about you going in before we have our people in place," Remy said. "Rafael and Landry did a thorough reconnaissance around the facility. Other than the guards on the exterior of the building, they didn't detect additional positions in a wider perimeter. We need to get our team in place, ready to take out the exterior guards before you and Lissette show up as Holly's parents."

Simon's gut clenched. "There are a lot of moving parts. I'm worried for Holly."

"Shelby should be there about now with the lab coats and communication devices. I'm on the way to the marina now. Our guys are converging there. We'll be set up with radio headsets. Shelby's also bringing you an array of weapons to choose from."

"I doubt they'll let us go in fully armed." Simon stepped out of the houseboat and crossed the gangway to the dock, anxious to get moving. "We'll take whatever we can get away with."

Headlights flashed at the end of the driveway, leading down to the houseboat.

"Shelby's here," Simon said. "We'll be leaving the dock within the next five minutes."

"Good, I'm almost to the marina now. Let's make this happen."

Shelby parked the Sheriff's department SUV and leaped out. With a handful of lab coats and a small duffel bag, she ran to the dock. The first items she pulled out were bulletproof vests.

Simon shook his head. "They'll frisk us, and those would be the first to go.

"Good point." Shelby handed them the lab coats.

They slipped into them quickly and buttoned the fronts.

Lissette's coat swallowed her, which would work in her favor as the people negotiating the exchange would expect an older woman to be a little thicker, not fashion-model thin.

Lissette glanced up at Simon and then reached to smooth his hair straight back. "That's more like a studious scientist. But if the guys who attacked you are there—which I suspect they will be—they'll recognize you immediately." She frowned and looked around. "You need glasses, a mustache and a hat. Anything to help disguise you."

"I have sunglasses in my vehicle," Shelby said.

Lissette nodded. "Get them."

Shelby ran up to her SUV and returned with sunglasses and a floppy fishing hat. "Found this in the back on the floorboard. I think it belonged to Bobby Smart. I brought him in the other day for drunk and disorderly conduct to sleep it off in one of our cells." She handed the hat and sunglasses to Lissette.

Lissette placed the hat on Simon's head and tugged it in place. Then she held up the sunglasses. "Nice sunglasses," she said, then grimaced. "Don't hate me for this." She punched the lenses out of the frame and handed the glasses to Simon. "Hopefully, they won't look close enough to notice there are no lenses." She stood back and studied him. "Better."

Shelby motioned to the duffel bag. "Choose your weapon."

"I already have mine." Lissette bent to pull up her pant leg, displaying a sheath with her bejeweled dagger tucked neatly inside.

Simon wanted to load up with a gun, several magazines full of ammunition and a couple of smoke grenades. His hand hovered over the K-Bar knife. Finally, he shook his head and stepped back. "Can't. They'll frisk us before they let us inside. They probably won't take offense to Lissette's knife, though they'll confiscate it. But if I go in with a weapon, they'll see it as a threat." He'd have to rely on his hand-to-hand combat training and the fact they wouldn't be expecting a scientist to jump them.

Shelby handed Simon and Lissette radio earbuds.

As Simon pressed his into his ear, a sheriff's boat drove up to the dock. Sheriff Bergeron waved from the helm.

"There's my ride," Shelby said. "Good luck."

Simon felt in his pocket for the rabbit's foot and remembered it was still in the wet jeans he'd left in the houseboat.

"I'll be right back." He ducked back into the houseboat, found the rabbit's foot and tucked it into his pocket. He was back on the dock seconds later.

"Ready?" he asked Lissette.

She nodded, her face set. "I'm ready. Let's go get

Holly. My pirogue or the skiff? Either way, I'm driving."

Simon's lips twitched. "Are all the Gautier women so..."

"Bitchy? Demanding? Cocky?" she offered.

"I was going to say confident and self-assured," Simon said.

Shelby laughed as she climbed aboard the Sheriff's vessel. "You have to have balls of steel to tangle with Voodoo Queen's spawn. *Bonne Chance*."

"We'll take the pirogue," Lissette said decisively. "The motor is quieter."

She climbed into the pirogue, took the cell phone with the map app open, so they could find the location they needed to reach, and waited silently while Simon settled into the middle seat.

Hand on the tiller, Lissette maneuvered the small craft out into the bayou.

Ridiculously aware of the damp rabbit's foot in his pocket, Simon prayed it truly was lucky and that it would help him get Holly out.

Alive.

CHAPTER 15

"The team is in place," Remy's voice sounded in Simon's ear as he and Lissette proceeded slowly, the BioEnergen facility in sight, the long pier where supplies had been brought in and product shipped out loomed ahead.

"Anton's drone is in the air with the infrared camera engaged," Remy reported. "As Rafael and Landry reported, there are no wide perimeter guards. Our guys have moved quietly and quickly into place, ready to take down the exterior guards as soon as you and Lissette are inside. One concern we have is the presence of a large yacht sitting a mile away, with a helicopter perched on the deck. We're trying to get a close-up of the registration decal to see who it belongs to."

"Let's hope Holly isn't on it," Simon murmured. "We're going in."

Lissette guided the pirogue to the pier and cut the engine.

Simon tied the line to a ladder and held the craft steady as Lissette eased out onto the ladder and climbed up to the pier.

Simon followed. Once on the pier, he looked around. It was empty—no people, no guards to walk them into the building.

He pushed the empty glasses frame up on his nose and held out his arm.

Lissette hooked her hand through the crook of his elbow.

"If I say drop or get down," he whispered, "don't hesitate. Hit the floor immediately."

Her hand tightened on his arm. "Holly's lucky she has you. You two are perfect together."

He didn't respond. He'd gone into this assignment convinced curses, magic and luck were just a bunch of hooey. However, the more he was around Holly and her family, the more he realized magic might be real. Now, when he needed it most, he prayed it was real.

As they neared the building, he spotted the first sign of life in the two guards, dressed in black, sporting military-grade weapons, helmets and flack vests.

They held their weapons at the ready until Simon and Lissette were within fifteen feet of their positions. Then one of the men pointed his rifle at Simon.

The other called out. "Halt."

Simon and Lissette stopped immediately.

"Identify yourselves."

Simon spoke first. "I'm Dr. Bastian Gautier. This is my wife, Dr. Evangeline Gautier. We're here for our daughter, Holly."

The man holding them at gunpoint remained still. The other set his rifle against the wall and approached the fake Gautiers.

Simon tensed until he was close enough that he could see his face. Simon relaxed a little. This guard wasn't one of the two men who'd attacked him earlier.

"You," the guard pointed to Simon. "Hold your arms straight out from your sides."

Simon did as instructed and held steady while the guard ran his hands over his shoulders and out to his wrists, then skimmed across his chest, under his arms, down his torso and all the way to his running shoes.

The guard straightened and moved to Lissette.

She immediately raised her arms out to her sides. The man ran his hands over her shoulders to her wrists, then across her chest.

She smacked his hands. "Excuse me!"

His eyes narrowed. "It's this or we do a strip search. Your choice, lady."

Lissette glared at him and raised her arms again. "You'd treat your mother this way?"

"Yes, ma'am," he said and continued his pat down, straightening after skimming over her left ankle, not bothering with the right one.

Simon released a quiet breath. They hadn't found her knife. Not that it was much of a weapon. He hadn't been completely sure what the guards would have done had they discovered it on her.

"Follow me," a guard said and turned. He gave the other guard a brief nod as he passed him.

That guard retracted his rifle to the ready position and stood fast at the door.

Once inside the building, they were led down a short hallway with doors on either side and out into what appeared to be a warehouse.

"We wait here," the guard said, coming to a halt in the middle of the cavernous space. Overhead lights were only partially lit, which thankfully left enough shadows that they might delay the moment of recognition a little longer.

"We came like they told us to," Simon said, hoarsening his voice to sound older. He also hunched his shoulders a bit to disguise their width. "Where's Holly?"

"Where's our daughter?" Lissette demanded, her voice strident. She sounded like a worried mother.

"She'll be released as soon as you're on board our research vessel," a voice said. A man stepped out of the shadows, dressed in tailored slacks, a black button-down shirt and a black blazer.

Simon recognized him as Marcus Solberg. Gunnar Reznik stood at his side. His heart skipped a beat, but Reznik's expression wasn't changing.

Simon hoped the dim lighting kept the fixer from recognizing him in his hastily assembled disguise.

"We aren't going anywhere until she's released," Simon said, his gaze sweeping the warehouse, counting the guards positioned in a semicircle around them. Five, plus Gunnar. Too many for Simon to take. He'd have to stall long enough for Remy and his team to secure the exterior and breach the interior.

"How do we know she's okay?" Lissette asked. "Show us proof of life."

Marcus snorted. "We don't have to do anything. You're here. As a matter of fact, we don't have to release your daughter. It might work more to our advantage to hold her until you unlock the file containing the formula for the bioenergy you were paid to produce."

"We aren't doing anything until you produce our daughter," Simon said. They had to know she was in the building, not on the so-called research vessel.

Marcus's mouth pressed into a thin line. "Fine." He lifted his chin toward Gunnar. "Get the girl."

Gunnar retreated through a door and reappeared, pushing Holly in front of him. As they neared Solberg, Gunnar gave her a hard shove, forcing her to her knees.

Simon steeled himself from reacting.

Lissette gasped. "Don't you hurt my baby."

Holly's eyes narrowed and then widened for a flash as recognition dawned. "Mom, Dad," she said, her voice shaky, "you shouldn't have come."

That's my girl.

"We couldn't leave you with these beasts," Lissette said.

"You don't abandon the ones you love," Simon said, his gaze connecting with Holly's.

In that moment, he understood the truth. He was in love with this brave, beautiful woman. It had happened so quickly, he hadn't recognized it for what it was. Seeing her being dragged away twice now had brought it home and made it so clear that he did not doubt what he felt. He loved Holly Gautier...Hazard...whatever she wanted to call herself.

"Exterior secure. Entering now," a voice whispered in Simon's ear. He'd almost forgotten the earbud. And it hadn't been part of the guard's frisking.

Lissette glanced his way, having heard the same.

"You have your proof of life, now open the damned file," Solberg said. "Jeffries, the laptop."

Dr. Harlan Jeffries stepped forward, carrying a laptop. "I'm sorry it's come to this," he said. "They threatened to hurt Celine if I didn't help them complete the formula. I tried, but you two did all the work. You're the only people who can unlock the file.

The laptop wants a biometric password." As he grew closer, his gaze met Simon's. His eyes widened.

Simon had to say something before Dr. Jeffries blew their cover. "I'm sure you did the best you could," he said, holding the other man's wide gaze. "The file is locked with a retinal scan. It takes both of us to open it."

Dr. Jeffries nodded but didn't say a word.

"Then open it," Solberg said, his impatience evident in his curt words and sneer. "We have buyers who expected delivery months ago."

"Number of bogeys with you?" Remy's voice asked in Simon's ear.

Simon cleared his throat. "It took us *six* years of hard work to create the formula. We had to protect our work from being stolen or weaponized."

Solberg snorted. "Fat lot of good that did you. Now, open the damned file."

Jeffries's hands shook as he held the laptop out in front of him.

"The retinal scanner only works if we get really close to the camera," Simon said, reaching out to the device.

"We're here," Remy said softly into Simon's ear.

"Be ready for when it opens," Simon said, his gaze going briefly to Holly, where she knelt on the floor. "You'll be amazed at what we've done."

"We'd better be," Solberg said. "Our customers are expecting big things."

Jeffries moved closer.

Simon laid his hand on the keyboard and leaned closer. Then he pressed hard on the keyboard, flipping the laptop out of Jeffries's hand. The doctor tried to recover it, but it was too late, and the device crashed to the floor.

At that moment, all hell broke loose in the warehouse. The sounds of booted feet, moving fast, echoed in the warehouse. Shots rang out. A couple of the guards fell to the floor.

"Get down," Simon yelled and pushed Lissette to the floor.

Remy's team moved in swiftly, weapons raised.

Holly kicked out, knocking Solberg off his feet.

Simon dove for Holly.

However, Gunnar reached her first, grabbed her by her hair and pressed the barrel of his gun to her temple.

Remy's team surrounded them. The remaining guards shared stunned glances, froze, then slowly lowered their weapons.

This left only Solberg and Gunnar still standing, with Holly between them. Dr. Jeffries was already on the floor with his hands beside his head.

Holly tried to lean her head away. "That fucking hurts." Suddenly, she spun and slammed her forehead into Gunnar's.

He released his hold on her long enough for her

to knee him in the groin and then throw herself to the side.

Simon stepped in and swung with all his strength, his fist connecting with Gunnar's nose.

The man staggered backward, blood gushing, his eyes clouding with tears.

Simon hit him again, this time with an uppercut to the jaw. The man fell backward, landing flat on his back.

Simon grabbed the gun out of his hand and stood over the fixer.

Remy's team had moved in to quickly subdue the other guards. Simon glanced around the space and noted Lissette moving behind Remy.

When Simon turned to Holly, his heart sank.

Solberg had an arm around her neck and a gun pointed at her temple. "If you want to see her alive again, I suggest you produce her parents. No more games." He backed toward a doorway, his arm firmly around Holly's neck. "For now, she comes with me."

Her face was turning red, which set Simon's blood pounding because he was holding her too tightly.

Then Holly went limp, the weight of her body dropping so fast it pulled Solberg off balance. To keep from falling over, he let go of Holly.

In a split second, Simon brought his hand up and fired.

Solberg's eyes rounded. He clutched at his chest

and fell to the ground, the gun skittering across the floor.

Holly lunged for it, turned and pointed it toward Simon. "Get down!" she yelled.

Simon dropped.

Holly fired.

When he turned, Simon found Gunnar teetering. The knife in his hand dropped, and then he folded like a rag doll and lay still.

A moan sounded from Solberg.

Holly went to him and pressed her hand to his chest. "I should let you die, but we need your testimony."

Landry hurried to take over, applying pressure to Solberg's wound.

Simon helped Holly to her feet and pulled her into his arms.

"I'm covered in blood," she protested.

"As long as it's not yours, I don't care." For a long moment, he held her, the rush of emotions so strong he didn't trust his voice.

Remy clapped a hand on his shoulder. "We have an ambulance on the way. The Sheriff's department has the research boat held up, and the Coast Guard's on the way."

Simon nodded, still holding Holly, an insane feeling overwhelming him that if he let go of her, she'd somehow die.

"Hey," she said, patting his back. "I'm okay."

"I know," he said. He was the one who wasn't okay.

She finally leaned back and cupped his cheeks in her hands. "You see? Your lucky rabbit's foot saved the day—along with my grandmother's gris-gris bag. We're alive. My parents are alive, and we defeated the curse."

He looked down into her eyes. "You're absolutely right. My life is blessed with magic."

She laughed. "What? A full reversal of the naysayer?"

He nodded. "I owe Johnny. He was right about the lucky rabbit's foot. It brought me to you. It made me lucky in love." He pressed a kiss to her lips. "That makes me the luckiest man alive."

She wrapped her arms around his waist and hugged him tight. "I know it's too soon, that things like this should take more time, but I don't care. I love you, Simon."

"I love you, too," he said and sealed his words with a kiss.

EPILOGUE

TWO WEEKS LATER...

"Here, let me hold that while you get out of the boat." Simon took the heavy pot of gumbo Holly had prepared for the first family potluck dinner they'd decided to hold since her parents had returned from the dead, her curse had been broken and everything was right with the community of Bayou Mambaloa.

Holly climbed out of the boat, wearing the colorful dress Gisele had given her, looking beautiful, fresh and happy.

Simon liked to think he'd put some of the smile on her face, especially after the night they'd spent making love.

He loved waking up with Holly in his arms and couldn't imagine a day without her in it. He'd even told her as much that morning when he hadn't been able to wait another moment and popped the question because the ring he'd purchased had been burning a hole in his pocket.

She hadn't even been disappointed that he hadn't done it "right" by planning a big proposal event, with a plane flying overhead, painting a smoke message in the sky that read, *Marry me.*

Nope, she'd been stirring the gumbo, wearing an apron over her dress, her hair up in a loose, messy bun. Still, the prettiest woman he'd ever seen. He'd gotten down on one knee and asked her to marry him before she wised up and figured she could do better.

She'd laughed and thrown her arms around his neck, shouting, *Yes!* And she'd been beyond excited to get to share the news with her family that afternoon at her grandmother's house.

Her feet firmly on the dock, Holly leaned up on her toes and kissed his lips. "I love you, Sinclaire Simon Sevier. I can't wait to marry you and live happily ever after with you."

"You know we still have to find a house," he said, wishing he could pull her into his arms and give her a proper hug and kiss, but the pot of gumbo stood between them.

"What do you think about buying the houseboat and renovating it the way we like?" She smiled up at him and lowered her voice to a whisper. "I kind of like the way it rocks when we're rocking the bedsprings."

SIMON

He laughed. "Actually, I was thinking the same thing. We can start with the deck where the fire was and work our way forward. Do you think LaShawnda would help us make the offer and do the paperwork?"

"I'm sure she would," Holly said, smiling down at her ring. We can plan our wedding for some time after we finish the renovations."

"Or before we start," Simon suggested.

Holly grinned. "I'm game. We don't need a big, fancy wedding. I'd rather spend the money on the houseboat."

They walked across the dock and up the rise toward the house where Holly's rapidly expanding family was gathered, along with a few friends.

They'd set up a line of tables, covered them with colorful plastic tablecloths and heaped them full of dishes with enough food to feed an army.

"Holly! Simon! You're finally here." Gisele hurried forward, took the pot of gumbo, set it in the middle of one of the tables and slipped a big ladle into it. "Come sit by me and Rafael," she said, and grabbed Holly's hand. "I saved a space for you and Simon." Then she glanced down at Holly's hand and squealed. "What's this! What's this rock on your ring finger?"

Holly's cheeks turned a pretty pink. "It's an engagement ring." She leaned into Simon. "Simon asked. I said yes. We're getting married."

Simon's chest swelled with pride at the excitement in Holly's voice. It matched his, which made it even better.

"Holly, my darling," her mother rushed forward and hugged her tightly. "Why didn't you tell us? When did this happen?"

Holly laughed. "This morning, in the middle of making gumbo."

Dr. Gautier held out his hand to Simon. "I couldn't be happier for my daughter and us. Welcome to the family."

"Thank you, sir. I'm pretty glad she said yes. I don't know what I would've done with the ring, otherwise." He winked at Holly.

She laid her hand in his. "You don't have to worry about it now. It's mine, and I'm not giving it back."

"Good. That means you're mine, and I'm yours. Life doesn't get better."

"Speaking of couples and engagements, did you see that Mitchell and Joyce got engaged?" Lissette asked.

"Oh, and Cody got a girlfriend," Gisele said.

"Cody?" Holly's eyes widened.

"He was visiting a friend in Bayou Miste and got knocked on his ass for coming on to a female game and fish officer. When he picked himself up, she told him to apologize and then had coffee with him. Apparently, she knocked some sense into him, and he liked it."

Holly laughed as they all took their seats. "I'm

happy for him." She smiled across the table at Joe, sandwiched between Madam Gautier and Lissette. "Hey, Joe. We're glad you came."

Her mother smiled. "Of course, he came. After hosting us for six months, Joe's family."

Joe nodded. "Thank you all for inviting me. I didn't realize how much I missed having company until Bastian and Evangeline moved out. I might have to rethink living off the grid."

"We'd love to see more of you," Evangeline said.

Simon tipped his chin toward Joe. "You might want to talk with Remy. The Bayou Brotherhood Protectors can always use good special operations men to protect the vulnerable and put the bad guys away."

"Speaking of bad guys…" Rafael lifted a bowl of potato salad and scooped a spoonful onto his plate. "Did you hear on the news that Marcus Solberg was arrested for Paul's murder and for attempted theft, treason and espionage?" He passed the bowl to Gisele. "He worked out a deal for a lighter sentence by implicating Secretary of State Edmund Carver in the whole affair. They'll both spend a significant number of years in jail."

"Where they belong," Gisele said.

Madam Gautier stood and tapped her knife against her glass of iced tea. "My dear loved ones, I'd like to propose a toast."

Everyone lifted their glasses.

"To my beautiful family, thank you for being the wonderful folks you are in your work, in your lives and in your hearts. And thank you to Simon and Holly, and to the people who had their backs and supported them while bringing my son and daughter-in-law out of hiding and back into the light. And I want to give a special thanks to my beautiful granddaughter, Lissette, for putting others before herself and showing the truth in her heart. I love you all so very much."

They raised their glasses. "To family!"

"And Lissette, Gisele and Holly, it will be my goal and pleasure to pass my knowledge of the Voodoo to you, who will use it in kindness for the good of others. We'll meet twice monthly and learn together."

Lissette beamed, Holly and Gisele smiled, and Simon worried about who they might target with jock itch.

As they finished their meal, Holly rose to help with the cleanup. Simon did his part as well.

"We'd love to stay longer," Holly said, "but we promised Mace we'd join the Bayou Reapers in their annual picnic with the single parents of the parish."

"They do a lot for the community," Gisele said.

"Oh no!" Lissette cried out.

All eyes turned toward her.

She held up the empty fishnet. "Napoleon's loose."

"Who's Napoleon?" Joe asked.

"The meanest rooster this side of the Mississippi River," Holly said. "He doesn't like men."

Simon shot a glance around, expecting the worst.

A sudden flutter of wings spun up beside him. He held out his hands to deflect the attack but caught the rooster instead.

Napoleon settled into Simon's arms as if he belonged there.

"What the hell?" Simon stared down at the rooster.

Madam Gautier nodded. "Good things happen to those who believe in magic."

If you enjoyed Simon's story look for
Maurice
coming soon!

CHILLED

A KILLER SERIES BOOK #1

New York Times & USA Today
Bestselling Author

ELLE JAMES

CHILLED

A KILLER SERIES

NEW YORK TIMES BESTSELLING AUTHOR

ELLE JAMES

CHAPTER 1

THE KILLING'S only just begun. Watch them drop now, one by one.

FOR THE PAST seven hours the words echoed through Brenna's head. No amount of loud music or talking to herself erased the sound, repeating like a mantra again and again.

When she finally slid her Jeep Cherokee into the driveway of the police station and parked on a hump of ice, she sat for a moment, letting the heater blow warm air in her face. If she had any strength left in her arms after the grueling drive, she would shake a fist at the sky.

Yesterday, she'd been fooled into believing spring had arrived with sunshine melting through the mounds of solid ice piled four feet deep outside her townhouse in Bismarck.

With a sigh, she switched off the engine, pulled her gloves on and wrapped a wool scarf around her face before she stepped out into the storm. The storm that had raged since midnight had dipped its subzero blast as far south as Des Moines.

A native of the northern prairie, she knew better than to count on spring arriving any sooner than April and usually not until May. Her eyes stung, and she pulled her scarf higher over her nose to ward off the bite of the icy wind. Still wired by her hair-raising drive from Bismarck in whiteout conditions, Brenna stomped loose snow from her insulated boots outside the door to the Riverton Police Station.

The weatherman had predicted snow flurries. However, one thing North Dakotans could count on was the unpredictable, harsh weather. A trip that usually took her three and a half hours had taken twice as long at half the speed.

In any other circumstance, she'd have waited to make the trip until the storm had passed and the road crew had worked its magic, clearing away the foot of snow already accumulated. The forty-mile-an-hour wind hadn't helped either. She'd struggled to see the road through the heavy snowfall and fought the gale-force gusts buffeting her four-wheel-drive vehicle all over the interstate highway. But she'd made it.

Stepping through the two sets of doors, Brenna

entered the police station. The reviving scent of brewing coffee filled her senses as she divested herself of the scarf and draped it over a hook, followed by gloves, stocking cap and, finally, her heavy parka. Even the short walk from her car to the building necessitated full snow gear unless she wanted frostbite. The coffee smelled even better without the wool filter around her nose, and she yearned to wrap her stiff fingers around a hot cup. But first, she needed to find Tom.

She planted her hands on the counter and leaned toward the curious young police officer. "Hi, I'm Brenna Jensen. Where can I find Chief Burkholder?"

"That you, Brenna?" a deep voice called out from a doorway beyond the front desk.

Her smile lifted upward as her mentor and old friend Chief Tom Burkholder stepped into the lobby.

When she held out her hand to shake his, he brushed it aside and engulfed her in a bear hug that forced the air from her lungs. God, it felt good to be home, even in such tragic circumstances.

Chief Burkholder set her away from him and stared down at her face. "Did you stop by to see your mother and sister yet?"

"Are you kidding?" She tipped her head to the side and back to loosen the muscles tensed in her shoulders and neck. "As soon as they assigned me to the case, I headed straight here."

"You're just like your father—all about the job. We sure miss him around here."

Her father had died of a massive heart attack two years after Brenna had joined the Riverton Police Department. He'd been so proud of his daughters' accomplishments, especially when Brenna had chosen to follow in his footsteps. Never once had he bemoaned the fact he hadn't had a son.

She missed her father. They'd understood each other, and he'd loved her unconditionally.

"Heard you're up for a new job in Minneapolis," the chief said.

"Yeah." A twinge of guilt nudged at Brenna, as if leaving North Dakota was the equivalent of a sin, when so many young people fled the state to find jobs. In her case, she had a job, but the new one meant an increase in pay and responsibility, with the downside of being farther away from her family.

"When do they make the final selection?" Tom asked.

"In a week and a half."

"I'll keep you in my prayers for the job and this case." He hugged her again. "You deserve the break." The chief dropped his hands, shoved them in his pocket and stared down at his feet. "In the meantime, things been happenin' around here."

"Did you find the women?" Brenna asked.

The chief shook his head, his skin almost as gray

as his hair. "No. We had dozens of state police and local citizens combing the countryside all weekend, but the storm...well, *you* know what it was like. We pulled them in as soon as the weather got bad. No use losing anyone else in that mess out there."

"Find anything in the victims' homes?"

"Nothing yet. Only thing we got to go on is—"

"—what the good ol' U.S. Post Office delivered directly to me," Brenna finished for him. Her mouth set in a bleak line. "I don't know what to make of it, but I sure as hell plan to find out."

"One other thing..." Chief Burkholder tugged at the tie already loose around his neck.

Brenna recognized the signs. Chief had more bad news he didn't want to tell her.

Her lips twisted into a faux smile, and she patted his back. "Might as well spit it out."

With a shake of his head, Chief Burkholder stared hard at her. "We had another woman from town go missing last night."

As if a heavy clamp pinched her lungs, Brenna fought to breathe normally. "Then the note is coming true. You sure she didn't go somewhere and forget to tell anyone?"

"No. Her car was still in her garage, her purse on the counter in the kitchen." The chief chewed on his lower lip. "And, Brenna, since victim number two was from East Riverton on the Minnesota side of the

Red River, we notified the FBI. They're taking charge of the investigation."

"Great. Let's hope they don't hamper our search like the last team they sent." She walked toward the coffee urn on the side counter and helped herself to a foam cup full of liquid resembling sludge. "I'm beginning to see what ol' Red McClusky meant when he said, 'We don't need no outsiders muckin' around our neck of the woods.' I just hope the hell they don't slow us down."

"I'm sorry you feel that way." A low, rumbling voice sounded over Brenna's left shoulder.

She froze. Then a wave of heat rose from beneath her turtleneck to fan out into her face. Inhaling deeply, she steeled her nerves and willed her cheeks to quit burning before she faced the voice. "Do you always sneak up on private conversations?"

"Only if it has something to do with the case I'm working." The man in front of her could have stepped out of an ad for an action-adventure cop movie. In his black leather jacket, black hair falling across his forehead, and eyes an intense emerald-green, he was too perfect to be true. The addition of a five-o'clock shadow only made him look better—a perfect male specimen, from a scientific viewpoint.

Science be damned. Brenna didn't need a perfect man making a mess out of this case. She didn't need distractions when women were being kidnapped and more than likely murdered in her hometown.

"Nick Tarver." He held out his hand without smiling or baring his teeth to soften the sharp lines of his face, only those intense eyes staring straight into hers. "I'd hoped for an amicable relationship with the locals while working this case."

"Special Agent Brenna Jensen, North Dakota Bureau of Criminal Investigations." *Not nice to meet you*, she added without voicing the sentiment. Maybe she was a bit touchy about the subject, but she didn't need another case screwed up by the FBI, or another physically faultless person in her life. Having her sister and her sister's husband thrown in her face at every chance her mother could get was already enough to make her want to scream. Why couldn't the FBI send a really ugly, capable agent instead of Nick Tarver?

AS NICK SHOOK HER HAND, he observed the way Brenna Jensen's forehead settled into a permanent frown. Instead of making her less attractive, she appeared like a fierce kitten ready to pounce on a wolf. And he was the wolf. He almost laughed until a pang of awareness registered in his libido.

This woman, who barely came up to his shoulder, with her straight sandy-blond hair and blue eyes, was like the girl next door. Fresh, clean and wholesome. Too small and vulnerable to be a cop. She was the kind of girl a guy could take home to meet his mother. Someone he might have liked knowing, if he hadn't already sworn off women. And as a potential victim, Brenna Jensen presented more of a liability than an asset to his case.

"Mind if I keep that?" She glanced down at the hand he still held and back up at him, her brows rising. "I'm sort of attached to it."

He jerked his hand away and stepped back, for a moment off balance and not liking it.

Brenna tipped her head toward the doorway leading to the rear of the building. "Show me where you're set up, and I'll show you my note."

"Not yet."

Her shoulders straightened, and she dragged in a deep, slow breath, as if preparing to go into battle. "What do you mean, not yet?"

"Before we do anything else, we need your statement."

The woman let the air out of her lungs. "On one condition…"

Tarver's brows dipped into a frown. He wasn't used to negotiating his orders. He opened his mouth to say so, but Brenna beat him to it.

"I keep my coffee." She gave him a saccharine-sweet smile.

His brows met in the middle before they straightened, and he nodded. She'd better not push him. He'd have her out of the building so fast—

Coffee in hand, she sailed toward the door leading into the back of the police station.

He hurried to follow her, falling in step behind her.

Before she'd gone too far down the hallway, she stopped so abruptly Nick bumped into her. Her body was soft and feminine, but beneath the layers of clothing, he could feel the steely strength of well-honed muscles.

Her mouth made a small O and then firmed into a straight line as she looked over his shoulder to the man behind him. "Interview room still in the same place, Chief?"

"You betcha," Tom Burkholder replied.

"Let's go, Tarver." With a dismissive glance, she resumed her pace.

"Nick. Call me Nick." He almost smiled at the cocky little she-devil's back. He preferred a woman with spunk—but not at work. At work, he liked people to follow orders. "Chief Burkholder will take your statement."

"Whatever. Let's get this interview over so we can get to work solving this case."

He stepped around her and led the way through a bank of desks to a room located near the rear of the building. He held the door as the chief entered and Brenna followed. As she passed close enough to touch him, Nick caught the scents of herbal shampoo and fresh snow.

A strange combination of winter and spring. The unbidden impression formed in his mind from just that little whiff, and he brushed it aside. That was too much detail about a witness he had no intention of keeping on his team.

Once they were inside the interview room, Nick Tarver closed the door, shutting them in and him out. He moved down the hall and stepped into the observation room to watch and listen to the interview through the two-way mirror.

Stark and plain, the room was basically empty, with only a heavy metal table and two folding chairs in the middle of the floor. A single, uncovered light bulb provided enough light to illuminate all four corners.

Brenna circled the room and stopped to stare into the mirror. "Hey, Agent Tarver, can you hear me? Because I don't want to repeat myself later."

He fought a sudden urge to chuckle. The woman was annoying, but ballsy.

Chief Burkholder waved toward a chair. "Have a seat, Special Agent Jensen." Gone was the surrogate-father figure, and in its place was the professional police officer.

She set her satchel on the floor and pulled out a photocopy of the note she'd received. "I suppose you'd like to see the copy of the note and the envelope…?"

He took the paper and shot a brief glance at it

before setting it to one side of the table. "Let's start at the beginning. Your full name."

"You know me, Chief." She glared at the mirror, her fingers tapping a rhythm on the tabletop.

She was impatient and possibly a bit nervous knowing Nick was watching her. He sat in a chair and crossed his arms over his chest. Good. Make her sweat. He was glad he'd chosen to watch instead of interrogating. This way he could study her openly.

The chief's lips twisted in a wry grin. "For the record, please. You know the drill."

With a sigh, she quit staring at the mirrored wall and stated, "Brenna Louise Jensen."

"Occupation—Special Agent for the North Dakota Bureau of Criminal Investigations?" the chief offered.

"That's right." She shot a defiant look at the mirror.

So, she was a criminal investigator. It didn't mean she'd work with him.

The older man wrote on a tablet and then looked up at her. "Tell me what happened."

"I found this letter in the mailbox at my townhouse when I got home from work on Friday."

Chief Burkholder sat up straight, his pen poised in midair. "Not at work, but at home?"

Nick leaned forward. That was news. He'd assumed she'd gotten it at her office. This meant the kidnapper knew where she lived.

She nodded. "Right."

"And there were no prints?" They knew there weren't any, but the chief had to put it into the record.

"No."

"Where was the letter postmarked?" the chief asked.

"Riverton Post Office." She sighed. "That's why I'm here."

"In your line of work, have you been assigned to cases involving violent criminals?"

Her chin rose as if challenging the man behind the wall. "Yeah. That's my job."

The chief scribbled her answers on the notepad before he looked up again. "And Riverton's your hometown, isn't it?"

"Yes, sir," she stated. "It's where I grew up."

The chief continued. "Has anyone from Riverton ever threatened you?"

"No," she said, her fingers drumming against the tabletop again.

"Were you ever involved in an incident that would make someone consider you a threat?"

Her hand stilled. "Other than my case work?"

"Correct."

She hesitated, darting another glance at the mirror as she tucked a long strand of hair behind her ear. "No."

Was the hair flicking a nervous gesture? Was she

not telling the chief something? Nick's gut said yes. What secrets could a criminal investigator have?

Chief Burkholder continued the questioning without delving into her answer. If Nick had conducted the interview, he'd have questioned her further. But she was a cop and probably didn't think the information was relevant to the case.

When the interview was over, Brenna stood and gathered her satchel and the copy of her note. "Now can we get on with solving this case?"

"Eager, aren't we?" The chief patted her shoulder. "Come on, I'll show you where they've set up."

Nick left the observation room ahead of Brenna and the chief and beat them to the large conference room. It had been converted to a "war room." Completely covering one wall was a large whiteboard with a timeline sketched out in black erasable marker. Three notches were marked with the names of the missing women and the times they'd been reported missing. Another spot was marked "Note."

Now that he had Brenna's statement, she wasn't necessary to the case, and Nick wanted her out of the station and on her way back to Bismarck.

Although she was another key to solving the case, Nick had no intention of allowing her onto his team. He liked to work with people he knew and trusted. Get in, solve the crime, get out and don't get involved. That was Nick's policy, and he sure as hell didn't want to be in this godforsaken, frigid country any longer than he had to. He braced himself for the coming clash of wills with Special Agent Jensen.

The woman topmost on his mind breezed into the war room and tossed her satchel onto the conference table as if throwing down the gauntlet.

Chief Burkholder handed Nick the copy of the note he'd already seen as a blurry faxed copy they'd received around four that morning while Jensen had been in route.

Nick laid the paper on the table and walked over to Brenna. No time like the present. "Thank you for your statement, Special Agent Jensen. We no longer need your services. I advise you to return to Bismarck and lock your doors."

She stared up into his face for a long moment, her rate of breathing increasing until the air she exhaled blew in a sharp stream out her nose. Then she stepped closer to him, until her chest bumped against his. "I'm an experienced investigator assigned to this case by the state of North Dakota. I'm not running from some jerk who thinks he can pull my chain."

"Agent Tarver," Chief Burkholder said and then cleared his throat. "Jensen is one of North Dakota's best."

"I don't care." Tarver's eyes never left her face, and his expression remained unflinching. "She's a liability. I can't focus on the case if I'm playing bodyguard."

Her face flushed red. "I don't need your protection. I've been in law enforcement for six years. I can take care of myself."

That she hadn't backed down impressed him at the same time it annoyed him. "In case you haven't gotten the picture, the FBI has jurisdiction and is calling the shots now. You're off the case."

"Understand this, Agent Tarver. I *will* be involved fully in this case, with or without the FBI. I have more at stake here than you or any of your agents. This is my hometown, not yours. Nobody gets away with kidnapping or murder in my hometown."

"Agent Tarver, Special Agent Jensen was assigned from the state level. She won't be returning to Bismarck. If you don't include her on the team, she'll work alone to solve this case. You'd better serve the cause by including her." Chief Burkholder laid a hand on Nick's shoulder.

Okay, so the girl had the chief's confidence. He could admire that, but he didn't like being forced to accept her on his team. He shook off the chief's hand and stared down his nose into Brenna's clear blue eyes. "Get this straight, Jensen, I give the orders. Do you understand?"

For a moment, he thought she'd spit in his eye and tell him to go to hell. But her shoulders pushed back, and she met his gaze head-on. "I do."

"Good. Then don't get in my way."

"So does that mean I'm a part of the team?"

"I'll let you know." For a moment, Nick swam in

the depths of her stormy blue eyes—until he remembered how badly he'd been burned by a woman with blue eyes and why he'd never go there again. "Time's wasting. We've got a killer to catch before he does it again."

Read more of Chilled

ABOUT THE AUTHOR

ELLE JAMES also writing as MYLA JACKSON is a *New York Times* and *USA Today* Bestselling author of books including cowboys, intrigues and paranormal adventures that keep her readers on the edges of their seats. When she's not at her computer, she's traveling, snow skiing, boating, or riding her ATV, dreaming up new stories. Learn more about Elle James at www.ellejames.com

Website | Facebook | Twitter | GoodReads | Newsletter | BookBub | Amazon

Or visit her alter ego Myla Jackson at
mylajackson.com
Website | Facebook | Twitter | Newsletter

Follow Me!
www.ellejames.com
ellejamesauthor@gmail.com

ALSO BY ELLE JAMES

Stealth Operations Specialists Series

Saint Nick (#1)

Rogue (#2)

Crusher (#3)

Draco (#4)

A Killer Series

Chilled (#1)

Scorched (#2)

Erased (#3)

Brotherhood Protectors International

Athens Affair (#1)

Belgian Betrayal (#2)

Croatia Collateral (#3)

Dublin Debacle (#4)

Edinburgh Escape (#5)

France Face-Off (#6)

Brotherhood Protectors Hawaii

Kalea's Hero (#1)

Leilani's Hero (#2)

Kiana's Hero (#3)

Casey's Hero (#4)

Maliea's Hero (#5)

Emi's Hero (#6)

Sachie's Hero (#7)

Kimo's Hero (#8)

Alana's Hero (#9)

Bayou Brotherhood Protectors

Remy (#1)

Gerard (#2)

Lucas (#3)

Beau (#4)

Rafael (#5)

Valentin (#6)

Landry (#7)

Simon (#8)

Maurice (#9)

Xavier (#10)

Jacques (#11)

Papa Noel (#12)

Everglades Overwatch Series
with Jen Talty

Secrets in Calusa Cove

Pirates in Calusa Cove
Murder in Calusa Cove
Betrayal in Calusa Cove

Raven's Cliff Series with Kris Norris

Raven's Watch (#1)
Raven's Claw (#2)
Raven's Nest (#3)
Raven's Curse (#4)

Brotherhood Protectors Yellowstone

Saving Kyla (#1)
Saving Chelsea (#2)
Saving Amanda (#3)
Saving Liliana (#4)
Saving Breely (#5)
Saving Savvie (#6)
Saving Jenna (#7)
Saving Peyton (#8)
Saving Londyn (#9)

Brotherhood Protectors Colorado

SEAL Salvation (#1)
Rocky Mountain Rescue (#2)
Ranger Redemption (#3)

Tactical Takeover (#4)
Colorado Conspiracy (#5)
Rocky Mountain Madness (#6)
Free Fall (#7)
Colorado Cold Case (#8)
Fool's Folly (#9)
Colorado Free Rein (#10)
Rocky Mountain Venom (#11)
High Country Hero (#12)

Brotherhood Protectors

Montana SEAL (#1)
Bride Protector SEAL (#2)
Montana D-Force (#3)
Cowboy D-Force (#4)
Montana Ranger (#5)
Montana Dog Soldier (#6)
Montana SEAL Daddy (#7)
Montana Ranger's Wedding Vow (#8)
Montana SEAL Undercover Daddy (#9)
Cape Cod SEAL Rescue (#10)
Montana SEAL Friendly Fire (#11)
Montana SEAL's Mail-Order Bride (#12)
SEAL Justice (#13)
Ranger Creed (#14)

Delta Force Rescue (#15)
Dog Days of Christmas (#16)
Montana Rescue (#17)
Montana Ranger Returns (#18)
Brotherhood Protectors Boxed Set 1
Brotherhood Protectors Boxed Set 2
Brotherhood Protectors Boxed Set 3
Brotherhood Protectors Boxed Set 4
Brotherhood Protectors Boxed Set 5
Brotherhood Protectors Boxed Set 6

Iron Horse Legacy

Soldier's Duty (#1)
Ranger's Baby (#2)
Marine's Promise (#3)
SEAL's Vow (#4)
Warrior's Resolve (#5)
Drake (#6)
Grimm (#7)
Murdock (#8)
Utah (#9)
Judge (#10)

Delta Force Strong

Ivy's Delta (Delta Force 3 Crossover)

Breaking Silence (#1)

Breaking Rules (#2)

Breaking Away (#3)

Breaking Free (#4)

Breaking Hearts (#5)

Breaking Ties (#6)

Breaking Point (#7)

Breaking Dawn (#8)

Breaking Promises (#9)

Hearts & Heroes Series

Wyatt's War (#1)

Mack's Witness (#2)

Ronin's Return (#3)

Sam's Surrender (#4)

Hellfire Series

Hellfire, Texas (#1)

Justice Burning (#2)

Smoldering Desire (#3)

Hellfire in High Heels (#4)

Playing With Fire (#5)

Up in Flames (#6)

Total Meltdown (#7)

Take No Prisoners Series

SEAL's Honor (#1)

SEAL'S Desire (#2)

SEAL's Embrace (#3)

SEAL's Obsession (#4)

SEAL's Proposal (#5)

SEAL's Seduction (#6)

SEAL'S Defiance (#7)

SEAL's Deception (#8)

SEAL's Deliverance (#9)

SEAL's Ultimate Challenge (#10)

Cajun Magic Mystery Series

Voodoo on the Bayou (#1)

Voodoo for Two (#2)

Deja Voodoo (#3)

Texas Billionaire Club

Tarzan & Janine (#1)

Something To Talk About (#2)

Who's Your Daddy (#3)

Love & War (#4)

Billionaire Online Dating Service

The Billionaire Husband Test (#1)

The Billionaire Cinderella Test (#2)

The Billionaire Bride Test (#3)

The Billionaire Daddy Test (#4)
The Billionaire Matchmaker Test (#5)
The Billionaire Glitch Date (#6)

The Outriders

Homicide at Whiskey Gulch (#1)
Hideout at Whiskey Gulch (#2)
Held Hostage at Whiskey Gulch (#3)
Setup at Whiskey Gulch (#4)
Missing Witness at Whiskey Gulch (#5)
Cowboy Justice at Whiskey Gulch (#6)

Boys Behaving Badly Anthologies

Rogues (#1)
Blue Collar (#2)
Pirates (#3)
Stranded (#4)
First Responder (#5)
Cowboys (#6)
Silver Soldiers (#7)
Secret Identities (#8)

Warrior's Conquest
Enslaved by the Viking Short Story
Conquests
Smokin' Hot Firemen

Protecting the Colton Bride

Protecting the Colton Bride & Colton's Cowboy Code

Heir to Murder

Secret Service Rescue

High Octane Heroes

Haunted

Engaged with the Boss

Cowboy Brigade

An Unexpected Clue

Under Suspicion, With Child

Texas-Size Secrets

Made in the USA
Monee, IL
25 November 2025